INCENSE

Crafting & Use
of Magickal Scents

About the Author

Carl F. Neal (Oklahoma) has been an incense maker for seven years. He conducts lectures and workshops and has written several self-published booklets on the topic.

To Write to the Author

If you wish to contact the author or would like more information about this book, please write to the author in care of Llewellyn Worldwide and we will forward your request. Both the author and publisher appreciate hearing from you and learning of your enjoyment of this book and how it has helped you. Llewellyn Worldwide cannot guarantee that every letter written to the author can be answered, but all will be forwarded. Please write to:

Carl F. Neal
℅ Llewellyn Worldwide
P.O. Box 64383, Dept. 0-7387-0336-2
St. Paul, MN 55164-0383, U.S.A.

Please enclose a self-addressed stamped envelope for reply,
or $1.00 to cover costs. If outside U.S.A., enclose
international postal reply coupon.

Many of Llewellyn's authors have websites with additional information and resources. For more information, please visit our website at http://www.llewellyn.com.

INCENSE

Crafting
&
Use
of
Magickal
Scents

CARL F. NEAL

2004
Llewellyn Publications
St. Paul, Minnesota 55164-0383, U.S.A.

First Edition
Second Printing, 2004

Book design and editing by Michael Maupin
Cover photo © 2003 by Leo Tushaus
Cover design by Lisa Novak
Interior illustrations by Kerigwen

Library of Congress Cataloging-in-Publication Data
Neal, Carl F., 1965 –
    Incense : crafting & use of magickal scents / Carl F. Neal. —1st ed.
        p.   cm.
    Includes index.
    ISBN 0-7387-0336-2
     1. Magic. 2. Incense—Miscellanea. I. Title.

BF1623.I52N43 2003   2003054535

Disclaimer: The remedies and recipes in this book are not meant to substitute for consultation with a licensed healthcare professional. Please use herbs within the guidelines given and heed the cautionary notes regarding potentially dangerous herbs. The publisher assumes no responsibility for injuries occurring as a result of herbal usages found in this book.

Llewellyn Worldwide does not participate in, endorse, or have any authority or responsibility concerning private business transactions between our authors and the public.

    All mail addressed to the author is forwarded but the publisher cannot, unless specifically instructed by the author, give out an address or phone number.

    Any Internet references contained in this work are current at publication time, but the publisher cannot guarantee that a specific location will continue to be maintained. Please refer to the publisher's website for links to authors' websites and other sources.

Llewellyn Publications
A Division of Llewellyn Worldwide, Ltd.
P.O. Box 64383, Dept. 0-7387-0336-2
St. Paul, MN 55164-0383, U.S.A.
www.llewellyn.com

 Printed in the United States of America on recycled paper

For my mother,
who taught me that all things are possible,

For Annette,
whose words of love and wisdom I can still hear today,

and

For Kelly,
who never doubted my abilities, although I often have.

Contents

LIST OF FIGURES

Acknowledgments

THERE ARE SO many people who have helped me that it's impossible to name everyone. I'd first like to say thank-you to those rare college professors who taught me far more than the class material. Dr. Biles, Dr. Merritt, and Dr. Perkins gave me the writing direction, the freedom of scope, and the research skills that have made this dream a reality.

Next, my thanks to the many patient teachers of the Craft who have illuminated dark places for me over the years. Although I've always been Solitary, the instruction and enlightenment I've gained from those far wiser in matters of magick has been invaluable. From personal conversations to public debates to workshops, all of you have helped me put the techniques of magick into simple words. My specific thanks to Annette and Mike Hinshaw for introducing me to the wider magickal community and for being my friends through many years of ups and downs. My thanks to both Mike and my great friend Kelly Killion for their labors in editing this book.

Thanks as well to David Oller from Esoterics LLC. His persistent persuasions took me off the road of artificial ingredients and convinced me that all incense should be wonderful and natural—not just ritual incense. Thanks as well to the hundreds of members of the numerous incense discussion groups (including David's) to which I belong. Your questions have been even more valuable to me than your answers. I hope that this book pleases you all.

INTRODUCTION

INCENSE MAKING IS as ancient as humanity's control over fire—older than written history and often shrouded in mystery. You now hold in your hands all the information you need to make your own incense from all-natural ingredients. From the simplest incense for daily use, to the most elaborate incense for rituals, with a few ingredients and this book, you can make any sort of incense you wish.

It's important to note that this book is not focused on making incense on a large scale. Most commercially produced incense is "dipped" incense that is far from a natural product. The making of dipped incense is barely mentioned in this book and certainly not explained. There are a few booklets in print about incense dipping, and you should consult those for information on making incense with synthetic materials. The focus of this book is making natural incense that is a blessing to its user.

How to Use This Book

To gain a full understanding of all the factors involved in incense making, you should read this entire book. But some people are anxious to "get their hands dirty," so here's a shortcut. Skim the rest of this chapter for a general introduction to incense. You should also skim over chapter 1, paying particular attention to the different forms of incense, and chapter 5 to see the basic tools you might like to use. Then carefully read chapter 6, and by the time you reach the end, you'll have made your first batch of incense! Once you've used a few recipes from this book, you should go back and read the rest of the book to further expand your knowledge.

What Is Incense?

Put simply, incense is anything you burn for its scent. That's a pretty broad definition, but it's accurate. Burning leaves are incense for some people, and firewood fits this definition for others. It doesn't take twenty-five secret herbs blended by a Japanese incense master to make fantastic incense. A few simple ingredients often make the most pleasing scents.

Why Burn Incense?

Humans are blessed with five basic senses. Of those, scent is, after touch, the most intimate. Most human senses have very complicated nerve processes that send information to the brain. Unlike the others, the sense of smell is "directly wired" to the brain. The left half of your brain controls your right hand, but your left nostril is connected to the left side of your brain. The sense of smell is an ancient trait and incense provides a quick connection to your brain. Memory and smell are heavily intertwined. Certain smells can transport us back in time to a memorable place or event.

Incense has many applications in life. Incense is a way to "redecorate" a room in seconds. Although it might take you days to paint a room in order to change how it looks, you can change how it smells by lighting a simple cone of incense. Not to mention that with incense, you can "redecorate" the room every thirty minutes if you so desire.

Incense is also a wonderful assistant for meditation. The gentle scents of sandalwood and cinnamon can bring greater depth to your meditation with the wonderful aftereffects of the lingering scent. In fact, many types of high-quality (and quite expensive) Japanese incense are an integral part of the meditation habits of people worldwide. This incense may actually create a biochemical reaction, which impacts the meditation experience.

As practitioners of ritual magick know, incense can make a tremendous difference to the entire magickal process. Incense is used to cleanse and create sacred space, as an offering both on and off the altar, a way to create a magickal atmosphere, and a way to help the practitioner achieve specific mental states. The effects of incense can have a deep impact on both major rituals and minor magick.

Finally, although it is quite mundane, sometimes there is a bad smell that you might want to mask. From litter boxes to cigarette smoke to stale fish, there are things in all our lives that don't smell as good as they could. Lighting up a stick of incense offers an immediate way to modify the scent of any room. It takes work and practice to make truly amazing incense, and it seems a shame to waste all of that energy on covering a bad smell, but incense exists to improve our lives. Bad smells detract from the joys of life, so using incense to change those smells is appropriate to improving our lives.

Why Make Incense?

Since there are so many brands of incense on the market, you might ask yourself why you should bother to learn how to make incense. There are numerous reasons, although any incense buyer can benefit just from understanding how incense is made. Making incense yourself allows you to avoid the problems of dipped incense, have complete control over the ingredients used, and allows you to greatly empower your incense. And best of all, it's fun.

Dipped Incense

You might have heard the terms "dipped," "soaked," or "double dipped" used to describe incense. This category of incense has changed in recent decades and is somewhat controversial. Dipped incense is made using incense "blanks." A blank is an unscented stick or cone of incense. The idea of dipped incense is fairly new in the long history of incense and in recent years the quality of dipped incense has come into question. Originally, these blanks were made of sandalwood powder and a type of glue. They are basically an incense "base" and "binder" (we'll talk in detail about those in chapter 2) that are rolled and dried. Instead of using plant materials to scent the incense, the sticks are soaked in oils. As the incense burns, the burning oils supply the scent. I personally have some concerns about the use of oils in general, but many people enjoy the benefits of essential oils on a daily basis. If you are comfortable with essential oils, then you can certainly use them in your incense.

So far, dipped incense sounds pretty nice. The problems come in from the practices in use by commercial incense makers. Essential oils are not used in making dipped incense. (There might be a few small producers who dip with essential oils, but I've never been able to locate any.) Synthetic fragrance oils are used instead. Currently, I am unaware of any health risk associated with pure synthetic oils, but a great deal of dipped incense is made with impure oils. Many commercial incense makers and oil sellers stretch their oil supplies by adding a so-called "extender" to their oil. The most commonly used extender is DPG, which is an abbreviation for "dipropylene glycol methyl ether." It is a chemical that adds little scent to the oil and can double or triple the amount of oil you have on hand. DPG is relatively harmless in its liquid state (although I still wouldn't have it anywhere near me), but may produce poisonous gas when burned! That's not something you should have in your incense.

In addition to DPG, incense blanks are not what they used to be. While blanks were once made from sandalwood or other appropriate woods, modern blanks are made using any wood powder at hand. Most blanks are made in countries with few or no regulations over them and might contain anything, including saltpeter or unhealthy adhesives. There's no way for the incense maker or user to know what material might be in that blank. In fact, you've bought blank incense sticks if you've ever used a "punk" to light fireworks—they are the exact same thing. Some experts have suggested that many incense blanks release dangerous chemicals themselves when burned (primarily formaldehyde), but I've never seen formal research that confirms that, so I'd take it with a grain of salt.

Obviously, few incense makers would use DPG or dangerous blanks if they understood these facts. The sad reality is that incense dippers can't even control these factors. Few people who dip could afford to have their blanks tested for dangerous chemicals. They might never add DPG to their oils, but they have no way of knowing if the company that sold the oil to them added DPG. Many wholesalers "cut" their fragrance oils in this way to increase their profits. Naturally, they never tell the incense makers who buy the oil from them. Do you have friends who don't use incense because it makes them feel ill or gives them headaches? The chemicals released by burning low-quality incense might be the culprit. Offer those friends some whole-herb incense that you made yourself and they might be able to enjoy it with no ill effects at all.

I don't want to give the impression that all dipped incense is a health hazard or is of lower quality. There are many dedicated incense dippers who would never intentionally cause harm. If dipped incense is made with a high-quality blank and only pure fragrance oils, it should present no danger whatsoever. It's simply impossible to know what quality dipped incense offers—even if you make it yourself.

Worse yet, the vast majority of dipped incense isn't made by dedicated individuals, but by foreign companies in the same nations that export blank incense to North America. They often manufacture their incense without regard to anything other than their profit margin. They aren't concerned with the problems that might result from their products. Although not universally true, you should definitely keep the hazards of dipped incense in mind any time you go shopping. Even "rolled" incense that you buy can contain dangerous chemicals since many incense makers still follow the poor practice of using saltpeter (potassium nitrate) and "cut" oils in their incense.

Control

All those hazards are a great reason to make incense yourself. The incense maker has control over chemicals like saltpeter or DPG, and when you make your own you can omit these hazardous substances. Beyond that, since you are the incense maker, you know about every single ingredient used in your incense. When you make your own incense, you can (and should) avoid ingredients that you dislike or that cause an allergic reaction.

Incense making also gives you far greater control over the ethical concerns of your incense. Most incense makers (myself included) never add animal products to their incense. Some incense makers prefer to avoid the use of rare ingredients out of respect for the Earth, while others feel it is the greatest way to honor Her. Making incense yourself gives you control over any ethical worries you might have. The ethical concerns of incense making are discussed in detail in Appendix C.

Empowerment

Another reason to make your own incense is purely magickal. Just as it's preferable to control the physical ingredients in your incense, the magickal ingredients are just as important. I'm talking about empowering incense. You can, of course, buy commercial incense and then attempt to empower (add magickal energies) to it. If the incense you're empowering is full of DPG or potassium nitrate, I don't see that empowering it would make it less offensive to nature, but you can always try.

Not only is it less effective to empower incense only after it has been made, you also have to worry about what kind of negative energies the incense might have collected. Most commercial incense is made overseas and sent to North America on cargo ships. It can take months for the incense to reach the shores of your nation. Then it can take months more before it appears on the shelf of your favorite store. During all that time, the incense has been exposed to many kinds of outside influences. When you buy incense, you don't even know under what conditions it was made. The energies of a poorly regulated factory might not be what you want to offer as a sacrifice to a God or Goddess of your path.

If you decide to make incense rather than buying it, you can empower it throughout the process. The ingredients you use have their own energies, but you can add to that power as you blend, mix, and roll your incense. You can empower it from start to finish. The result will be incense that you feel honored to offer on your altar. No matter how wonderful commercial incense might be, it is impossible to surpass the power of incense you make your-self for magickal uses. You can focus your intent for the incense (love, health, prosperity, etc.) through the use of visualization. That is discussed in more detail in chapter 2.

Enjoyment

There are still more great reasons for making your own incense. If you are an avid user of incense, then learning how it is made is important to you as well. Even if you never intend to make a single stick of incense, this book will give you the knowledge you need to be an informed consumer. You will have a basic understanding that will allow you to be much more critical when buying incense.

Perhaps the single most important reason to make incense is that it is fun. It's a simple thing to say, but the process of making incense is joyous. Burning your incense is a second chance for it to bring you joy. If you have no desire to make incense for ritual use, then make some just for the fun of it—you won't be disappointed!

The World of Incense Making

As soon as you make your first batch of incense, you will join a line of incense makers that stretches back beyond the boundary of written history. Although the earliest incense mak-ers undoubtedly made "loose" incense that was burned in or over a fire, no one can guess how long mankind has enjoyed the benefits of incense. As you make incense, think of that line of women and men that stretches back further than anyone can see. This is an ancient art that we can continue to explore in the modern world. This will be the quickest history lesson you've probably ever had, but I want to give you a sense of how this ancient art has come into this new century.

India

India is the home of many of the basic materials used in incense making. With mate-rials ranging from fine sandalwood to the Goddess Myrrh, India has long been the home of master incense makers. Although fine Indian incense is difficult to locate in North America, many basic incense traditions come from that distant land. The majority of incense from India in the twenty-first century is of the dipped variety, discussed earlier.

You may have heard of the "Silk Road," or the "Spice Road," but the trade in Indian spices was just as much a trade in aromatic incense ingredients. Among the many goods that trekked across continents were frankincense, myrrh, sandalwood, and camphor. Not only did India offer the world its goods, but it offered its incense traditions as well. The trade routes went west of India all the way to Europe's western shore, and east to China and beyond.

China

China has long been a land where all aspects of life were closely observed and studied. Herbs, teas, and incense itself were all subjects of careful consideration by skilled Chinese artisans. As the Chinese worked to improve and perfect their skill with fireworks, they did the same with incense. It is believed that China was the birthplace of the incense stick (what I call a "spaghetti stick"), which is the ultimate form of incense. The innovation of "self-burning" incense (doesn't require an outside heat source) truly elevated incense making to an art.

Although China is also primarily a maker of factory-produced dipped incense, quality incense is still produced there. Unfortunately, there is no good source for this incense in the West, but changes in China might offer us access in the future. From China, the skills of the incense maker continued to move east to Japan.

Japan

Although certainly not the creators of incense, the Japanese are arguably the world's incense making masters. In Japan, the art of incense making was taken to unequaled heights. Even today, traditional Japanese incense masters study their entire lives. Tens of thousands of hours are needed to learn enough to become such a master. Even though the introduction of new ingredients is rare, these masters are able to create incense that is the result of the life's work of dozens of masters who came before.

We are fortunate that we are able to buy several brands of this high-quality Japanese incense in the West. It is important to note that just because incense is labeled "Made in Japan" does not mean that it is the high-quality incense mentioned. High-quality incense is generally quite expensive and is, not surprisingly, more difficult to locate than some of the lower-quality incense from Japan.

Europe

Europe also has a very long history of incense use. The primary difference between the East and West is that Europeans didn't make the transition to self-burning incense. European traditions, from the censers of ancient Greece and Rome to the fires of the Celts in the west, grew into their own body of knowledge. The ingredients from the Far East were incorporated into this lore, but all of the local flora was included as well. Although demeaned in some corners of the modern incense making world, European incense traditions are rich with understanding of the Earth and Her power. That is an understanding sometimes lacking in other traditions.

The New World

Although less well-known, North and South America also provide valuable contributions to our incense traditions. From Mayan copal smoldering with the blood of a high priest to the Incan burning of palo santo wood, the New World offers us a variety of incense-making materials not available in the Old World. In North America, deer's tongue (it's a plant, not an animal part), desert sage, pine, and even tobacco are part of the incense tradition. These materials are all at the disposal of modern incense makers.

In ancient times, the world was crisscrossed with trade in valuable aromatics and spices. Although products of the New World were limited to North and South America until the sixteenth century, in modern times we have access to a wider range of aromatics than ever before, and modern trade has made many of the once rare materials common and affordable. At times, frankincense has been more valuable than gold (and anyone who has enjoyed frankincense understands why), but today it is quite affordable to people of virtually any income level.

The Philosophies of This Book

Every nonfiction book, especially one of this nature, is written with certain philosophical perspectives. The methods that I describe in this book aren't the only methods or approaches that will work. I don't offer this book as the "final word" on incense making. Rather, I see it as a first step to wider understanding. If you disagree with an approach or a philosophy in this book, then I invite you to challenge it. Only by having open discussions, research, and debate can we improve both our techniques and basic approaches.

Many practitioners of ritual magick have already received specific training with incense. Different traditions follow different methods and philosophies. If you find that what I say conflicts with that training, follow the teachings of your tradition. I mean no disrespect to those who follow different philosophies and hope that we can show each other new ways. The following are a few of the methods I use.

The Whole Herb Method

Making "whole herb" incense is a fairly new concept to me, but I am a strong proponent of it. Whole herb incense is made only from natural plants, resins, and woods. In general, whole herb incense avoids the use of oils—including essential oils. The whole herb approach stresses using plant material over the use of oils. Rather than using lavender essential oil, you would use lavender flowers. Replace patchouli oil with a patchouli leaf. Essential oils are distilled from plant material and are subject to chemical changes during the process. The whole herb contains the oil in its natural form. Since this is a book for beginners, I have not included oils in any of the recipes.

Using Oils in Incense

Although I prefer the whole-herb method, I do understand that a lot of people enjoy using oils in their incense. Oils are little mentioned in this book, but you will see that the chapter on rolling incense does tell you when it is appropriate to add the oils to your mix. If you plan to use more than one type of oil in your incense (perhaps a mixture of ylang-ylang and cassia), you should mix the oil several days or weeks in advance. Combine them in a glass or ceramic container. Once or twice a day you should shake or stir the oils again. After a few days, they will begin to merge their scents and can then be added to your incense dough. Oils can be added to your incense once your dough is ready to roll. The use of oils in incense can be a complex issue. I may discuss it in-depth in a future book, but for now I would say use oils if you feel comfortable with them and have confidence in your knowledge about them. I occasionally use oils in incense, but in general I make whole-herb incense.

The Dry Mix Method

This book also emphasizes the "dry mix" method. This method brings together all of the dry ingredients, including the binder. Water (or another liquid) is added and then the incense is rolled. There are other incense makers who favor the "wet method" where the binder and the water are mixed first and then the other ingredients are added. The wet method will work for most of the recipes in this book, but I don't go into any detailed explanations as to how to do that. I find the dry mix method to be easier, less messy, and more precise—especially for novice incense makers. But if you are more comfortable or have experience with the wet method, then certainly feel free to use it instead.

Traditional Recipes

I want to distinguish this from the magickal traditions that I just discussed. I don't mean a magickal tradition (sometimes called a "path" or "system"). In many books (and in many places on the world wide web) you will find "traditional" recipes. Any time in this book you see the word "traditional" in quotation marks, I'm talking about these recipes that are rarely traditional at all. Many times the "tradition" of such recipes goes back a whole ten or twenty years. Many of those recipes also call for unusual ingredients collected in strange ways (flowers collected by a running brook on an odd number weekday). Such things are most frequently found in recipes meant to dissuade would-be magickians and aren't a real requirement. It is true that gathering plants under a full moon or on the equinox, etc. can intensify the power in your ingredients. Just beware of any recipe that's marked "traditional" unless you have a great deal of faith in the source of the material. Also be aware that even real traditional recipes might contain products that are no longer available or are ethically questionable. I suggest that you substitute more appropriate materials.

The Evils of Saltpeter

I also want to warn you about an old practice that needs to be avoided. Many books about incense making (including some quite good ones) advocate the use of saltpeter (potassium nitrate). I urge you not to follow this practice. Incense that won't burn without saltpeter in the recipe should be reformulated. Properly formulated incense will burn without the use of this harmful chemical. Not only does it add an unpleasant scent to your incense, it will also change its magickal energies. Saltpeter is under the sign of Fire, so if it is used in all incense you will slant all your work toward that sign. If Fire is at cross-purposes with your magick, it might harm you more than help. On top of all that, saltpeter is a hazardous material. You can't legally send it through the mail or ship it with most package services without paying large additional fees. I know that some companies sell it without taking this extra precaution, and that poses a hazard to the carriers. It's dangerous to have it in your house and I urge you never to include it in your incense.

Experimentation

The final philosophy that I want to explain is about experimenting. There are many incense "experts" who feel that experimentation should be left only to the most skilled incense makers. They feel that, first, experimentation will never yield as good a result as the incense you can purchase from high-quality suppliers. Second, they believe that incense making is quite powerful and in untrained hands could be a hazard. I find the chances of that quite remote. Experimenting is the only way to learn and explore, and incense is a subject that merits exploration. It's also the only way to use your local incense ingredients that aren't discussed in any books. If you feel uncomfortable with experimenting, that's fine too. The recipes in this book will offer you a wide enough range of recipes to keep you entertained for years.

Incense making is an ancient tradition that extends well beyond humanity's memory. Becoming an incense maker is as simple as continuing to read this book, but you will then be a part of a legacy that is older than writing. Most importantly, making incense offers you a chance to make a spiritual connection with nature that can't be found any other way. The ability to empower your incense from start to finish, make incense that is natural and pure, and to make an intimate connection with your finished product (a connection that isn't possible with commercial incense) are all great reasons to make incense. Just don't forget—it's fun, too!

THE IMPORTANCE OF FORM

ALTHOUGH MOST AMERICANS are only familiar with incense cones and sticks (with bamboo rods), incense comes in a variety of forms. It might not seem that important at first thought, but the shape will have a huge impact on how well your incense burns and the required tools. You will need to carefully consider the form of your incense not only to improve its combustibility but also to properly incorporate it into your rituals.

Loose Incense

This is certainly the oldest form of incense burning. Born in the camp-fires of the ancients, the practice of adding aromatic plants and woods to a smoldering campfire surely marks the birth of incense. "Loose" incense, unlike sticks or cones, is not a "self-burning" form. That is, you must supply heat to loose incense or it will stop burning.

In modern times, the most common way to do that is by using charcoal tablets inside an incense burner. Incense burners for loose incense (called "censers") will be discussed in detail in chapter 3, but charcoal deserves some comment here. Most people who burn loose incense use "self-lighting" incense tablets. These are round charcoal tablets that usually have a round impression in the center. The impression is used as a crude bowl to hold the aromatics you place on the charcoal. Manufactured by several different companies, they bear a variety of brand names. If you enjoy burning loose incense, I would urge you not to use this type of charcoal. This type of charcoal is "self-lighting" because it is full of saltpeter. After holding a flame to one edge of the charcoal for fifteen to twenty seconds, the charcoal will begin to spark and sputter. A burning line will move over the surface of the charcoal and then the tablet begins to glow. That's the saltpeter. It makes them easy to light but it also makes them burn too hot and smell very bad.

If you use this type of charcoal, try this experiment. Light your charcoal as you normally would, but don't put anything on it. Don't use a lid over your censer or use a censer that is dirty. Allow the charcoal to burn by itself for two to three minutes while you sit far away from it. Go back to the censer and smell. If you smell a pleasant aromatic, your censer probably has some leftover oil or resin on it. More likely you will smell a subtle but quite foul odor. That is your charcoal. That scent is added to anything you burn on that charcoal. Ninety percent of that smell comes from the saltpeter in the charcoal.

Does this mean that you shouldn't burn incense on charcoal? Definitely not! As you'll see later, this form of burning is useful to all incense makers. It allows you to test new aromatics and new blends without devoting the resources to rolling incense. The good news is that there are two different solutions to this problem. The first, and in my opinion the best, solution is to stop using self-lighting charcoal. Instead, switch to bamboo charcoal. This type of traditional Japanese charcoal is made without the use of saltpeter. It is a little more difficult to light than the "self-lighting" type of incense (and it's more expensive), but you'll find the results well worth the effort. This charcoal has only the faintest scent and will have a minimal impact on the scent of any aromatics you might burn on it. To totally eliminate the smell of the charcoal you can burn "kodo style" (see Appendix E). A second Japanese method to avoid self-burning charcoal is "makko burning" (also discussed in-depth in Appendix E), but personally I hate to see anyone waste makko like that, so I'd suggest finding bamboo charcoal.

Loose incense is a great technique, but it has a number of drawbacks. The primary one is that it is not self-burning. Even if you switch to high-quality bamboo charcoal, you still need the charcoal, a censer, ash or sand, plus the incense itself. Conversely, you can drop a cone of incense into your pocket and light it up anywhere you go. That's much simpler than loose incense. Smoke is another problem. You have less control over the amounts of smoke produced. Novice users in particular tend to add too much material to the charcoal and raise huge plumes of smoke. Charcoal that contains saltpeter burns very hot and will burn a great deal of material very quickly, so you need to keep replenishing the incense if you want continuous burning. This is also true of other types of charcoal.

All incense makers should learn to burn loose incense. It was the first form and is still quite useful. It just isn't convenient to use. It is far easier to carry a little self-burning incense with you than everything required for loose incense. You also get control over the amount of smoke. Keep these tools around for experimentation. I won't talk much about the composition of loose incense in this book. There are many books on the market that discuss this form of incense in-depth. In fact, most New Age books that have "incense" in the title only discuss loose incense or only vaguely talk about self-burning incense, so I'll leave the details of making loose incense to them.

3

Sticks with Bamboo Rods

This is the form that most Americans think of when you mention incense. These days, even grocery stores and pharmacies carry nationally known incense brands. Many people like this form of incense, but I consider it the worst form. Have you ever wondered why the incense has that stick up the middle? Does it help the incense burn? No, in fact it frequently stops the stick from burning. In fact, there are two types of incense that use bamboo sticks. The first are rolled incense. This is rare, but not unheard of. Some natural incense is quite weak and won't stand on its own even when dry. It is wound around the stick for support. Some people also roll incense and then insert a bamboo stick into the stick (at least one major producer does this).

Much more commonly, the stick in question began life as a "blank" incense stick and oil was then added to it. The vast majority of commercial incense is made in this fashion. This type of incense is easy to make. Unscented "blanks," which are what you get if you buy "punks" at a fireworks stand, are soaked in synthetic fragrance

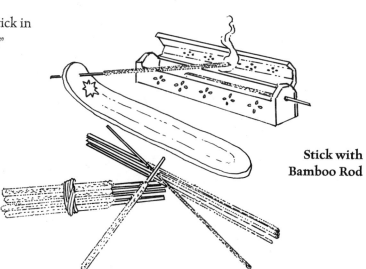

Stick with Bamboo Rod

oils. Most of the sticks (and even cones) on the market are made this way. Certainly not all, but the great majority (including all the most popular brands). Personally, I prefer natural incense and avoid burning this type of incense. Hopefully you will too once you've read this book, but if not then at least you will understand what you're buying.

Regardless of which reason incense has a stick, the stick itself offers a drawback. Sticks of bamboo like that don't want to burn. Light the end of a bamboo skewer and blow out the flame. It glows for a moment and goes out. Therefore your incense has to burn well enough to not only burn itself but that bamboo rod as well. If you're making natural incense that needs the support, use the sticks. Otherwise, do yourself a big favor and forget the bamboo rod.

If sticks are so bad, why are they created in the first place? The primary reason is physical strength. That bamboo rod makes the incense much more durable during shipping. The finer forms of incense are more prone to breakage than incense with bamboo rods. Keep in mind that most incense sold in North America is made in India. Even the bulk of incense made in North America is produced using Indian or Chinese incense blanks.

Cones

The cone is a relatively recent development in incense making. It is just over a hundred years old and was also created for shipping durability. Unlike the stick, however, the cone is a boon to incense makers. Cones are durable and, when made correctly, burn well. The cones that are available commercially are often of a very poor shape, so I wouldn't advise trying to duplicate them. A cone needs to be tall and thin but most commercial cones are short and stout. That makes them harder to break but also harder to burn. Commercial incense makers most often overcome this problem by drenching them in oil (incense "dipping"). If you put enough oil on them, any shape of cone will burn.

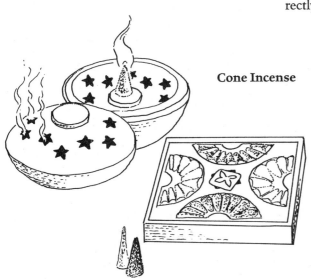

Cone Incense

Cones are a great form for several reasons. First, they are easy for even first-time incense makers to create. The shape can be formed very roughly and still burn or it can be very refined. Cones can also be molded. They are relatively durable, so you can carry them in your pocket. Making a burner for a cone is as easy as finding a discarded soda can or even just putting a nickel on a rock. If you roll cones by hand, each one will have a distinctive look. Molding tends to give you a more commercial uniformity. Just be aware that rolling successful cones is slightly trickier than thin cylinders.

5

Spaghetti Sticks and Cylinders

This is the ultimate form to give to your incense. Cylinders are essentially round rods of incense material. They can range in thickness from the size of a pencil down to the thickness of a toothpick. Cylinders generally offer the best burning properties and maximize your chances of successful incense making. The thinner the cylinder, the better its burning properties.

This form of incense is also called a "joss" stick. I call cylinders the thickness of spaghetti or thinner "spaghetti sticks." You'll see I use that term throughout this book. Spaghetti sticks are the very best form of incense for most purposes. They will burn better than any other shape. In fact, you might find that some of your recipes won't burn in any other form. They are easy to light and can be made in any length. The only real drawback to the spaghetti stick is that they are more fragile than other forms. Spaghetti sticks can be rolled to size by hand or extruded (for details on extruding see chapter 6). You can also make square "cylinders." You might even occasionally see commercial sticks that are square. Those are easy to make by rolling the incense dough flat and cutting the sticks rather than rolling them individually.

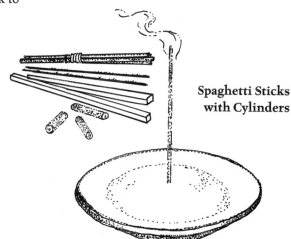

Spaghetti Sticks with Cylinders

Coil Incense

The incense coil is a slightly modified version of the spaghetti stick. Rather than leaving the stick straight, you can circle the incense around in an ever-widening spiral. This is another very old form, long understood in the East. The great advantages of coil incense are both the burning time and the small storage area required. A spaghetti stick can be made quite long, but the longer they are the more prone they are to break. A spaghetti stick that is three feet long is the practical limit. Such a long stick would be extremely difficult to store safely and would need a three-foot-long storage box. Whereas a coil made from a three-foot-long spaghetti stick will only require about nine square inches to store. By coiling incense, you can make a single piece of incense as long as you'd like.

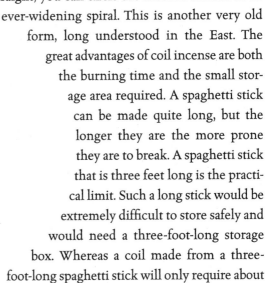

**Coil
Incense**

6

Other Forms

While wet, incense is a lot like wet clay. It can be formed into virtually any shape desired. That gives the incense maker a lot of flexibility and allows for some creative efforts. The incense disk is one fun form. I once supplied a Sunday school class with enough material to make fifty incense disks with frankincense. Rather than burning the incense, they made disks and put a small hole through the top. They then slipped a string through the hole and the kids were able to wear the incense! I've made disks like this with groups myself and it was a lot of fun. Most incense will warp a little as it dries, so disks don't usually stay flat but they are a unique way to show off your incense making skills. If made thin enough, most incense will burn in disk form. Alternately, you can break pieces from the disk and burn those instead.

In addition to the simple disk, you can buy inexpensive cookie cutters and cut your wet incense dough into any shape you desire. The shape might not completely burn, but they often do. Most people never even light novelty incense of that nature. They usually keep it intact. You'll find that you can have a lot of fun with wet incense.

Another unusual form of incense is "moist" incense (also called "kneaded" incense). This is incense that will never completely dry. There is a very famous Egyptian Kyphi incense recipe that has been reprinted in many books on the subject. It is made with honey as a binder and is intended to be kept wet and burned over charcoal. In Japanese moist incense is known as "nerikoh." It is made using honey or plum meat and is actually aged in a sealed contained that's buried from several months to several years. Moist incense is a truly unusual form and was an important step to making self-burning incense. It's also a lot of fun to make.

Since incense dough is so easy to work with, you'll find that you can make most anything from it. You're only limited by your own artistic skills. From log cabins to abstract sculpture, you can use cylinders as construction material or you can form lumps of incense dough into the desired shape. There are two important tips I'd offer to the creative incense maker. First, don't start out trying to craft sculpture. Learn to make good incense first, then try your hand at sculpture. Second, try to use thin strips of incense if you plan to eventually burn your work of art. If building a cabin of incense, for example, keep the various layers of "logs" separated from the layers above. You don't want all the logs burning at the same time or you'll create a mass of smoke. Not to mention that your creation will burn very quickly. Wax paper works well to keep layers from sticking together while they dry.

Other Incense Forms

Choosing a Form

In addition to understanding the strengths and weaknesses of each form, there are a few other factors to consider when choosing which form of incense to make. You should keep in mind that each batch of incense dough can be used to create more than one form. You can divide your dough into parts and create some cones, some spaghetti sticks, and some coils (or whichever combination you prefer).

The first factor you need to think about is the tools and workspace available to you. If you want to make extruded sticks, for example, you'll need an extruder. If you want to make molded cones, you'll need a mold. You can make spaghetti sticks (or even thick cylinders) that are over twelve inches long, but do you have a drying board large enough to hold a stick that long? Coils and cones require the least amount of space both to make and to dry.

The next factor to consider is how you intend to use the incense. Will you require a long burning time or will a short one do? Keep in mind that the burning time of your incense is primarily determined by its length. The longer your incense (or the taller the cone), the longer it will burn. Thicker incense will burn a little slower than thin, but be wary of making incense that is too thick. Thick incense tends to go out—never make incense thicker than an unsharpened pencil. You also need to think about where the incense will be burned. If you plan to use it outdoors, you might want to consider making sticks with bamboo rods. If you need a long burning time but only have a small space for the incense, then a coil might be the perfect choice.

Finally, if you're making incense for ritual purposes you need to consider both your own ritual practices and the specific spell work you're planning. How do you use incense on your altar? (For specific suggestions on this topic, see Appendix D.) If you normally use a censer and loose incense, you might consider leaving at least a portion of your dry-mixed incense in powder form. Just put some aside before you add liquid to it. If you plan to use cone or stick incense, do you have an appropriate burner that you feel comfortable using on your altar? What kind of incense would best suit your planned spell work? If your spell calls for only one blend or aromatic you might want to make a single long stick or coil. If it calls for the use of different aromatics at different points of the spell you might want to make a series of small sticks or cones and then light each one at the appropriate time. With your new understanding of using and making incense, you might even rework your spell to incorporate your new wisdom.

Incense can be shaped in a wide variety of ways. From the humble cone to the longest coil, it all offers us pleasure and energy. The shaping of incense is a great opportunity to let your creative energies flow. Considering the form of incense you wish to create takes an understanding not only of the forms themselves but also of the intended use and magickal purposes of the incense. Personally, I like to make incense in many different shapes and forms. Try them all and find the ones that suit you the best.

CHAPTER TWO

INCENSE COMPOSITION

THERE ARE MANY different ways to look at incense composition. I am certain that many traditional views of how incense is made might see the subject in a different light, but this method works well and is very simple. For the purposes of this book we'll look at incense as made up of three physical parts: aromatic, base, and binder. The final, nonphysical, component is its magickal aspect.

Aromatics

The aromatic is the part of the incense that primarily supplies the scent. Any plant, resin or wood can be used as an aromatic as long as you like its scent when it is being burned (and you can be reasonably certain it is not harmful). Many "traditional" incense blends call for unpleasant or unsafe materials as aromatics, so I offer this important guide: if it stinks, don't use it. If you find an incense recipe that calls for patchouli and you don't like patchouli, don't use it. If you find a recipe that calls for lavender flowers and you are allergic to lavender, don't include it regardless of its magickal properties.

Does that mean you should only use aromatics that smell wonderful by themselves? Not at all. It is sometimes surprising that an aromatic with a very strong or unusual scent alone may add well to another scent when used carefully. Many aromatics don't smell all that great when burned alone (turmeric for example) but can add a wonderful scent when used in combination with other aromatics. Some aromatics are very strong and need to be used only in small quantities (dragon's blood for example). They smell wonderful when used in the proper proportions but can be overwhelming if too much is used. Sometimes with careful blending you can even simulate one scent with a combination of totally unrelated scents. I have a blend with red cedar and myrrh that smells surprisingly like cinnamon.

To test an aromatic, always burn it. When you open a bag of frankincense you are greeted with a wonderful rush of fragrance, but that's no guarantee of the scent you'll have when it is burned. By the same token, if you open a bag of myrrh granules you'll smell very little. Even in powder form myrrh has very little scent. Once you add heat to it, however, you are greeted with a wonderful warm scent that is hidden in the resin. This is releasing the Goddess in the smoke. Testing by burning is the only way to know with certainty how an aromatic will smell while being burned in your incense. It's a good idea to test your incense blends before rolling too, but it certainly isn't mandatory.

There are a couple of ways to burn your aromatics. The traditional way to do this is by burning the aromatic on charcoal. This is an excellent method, but don't forget the warnings about "self-lighting" charcoal from chapter 1. If possible, use high-quality bamboo charcoal for your testing (see Appendix E). This is the most common way that incense is burned in rituals, so the tools to do this are very easy to find (or even make for that matter).

If you don't want to use charcoal, you can also use an old pan or skillet (don't forget, once used for incense you can't ever use it for food again) over a very low heat on your stove. Alternatively, you can hold a small strip of metal over a candle flame and test aromatics that way. Make certain that you hold the metal with pliers or some other tool, otherwise you could easily burn yourself on the hot metal.

A final note about burning. No matter which method you use, once the aromatic is burned, remove it from the heat. You can leave ashes on charcoal and continue to heat them long after they have burned. The resulting smell can be very unpleasant. You don't have to worry about that happening with your self-burning incense. Charcoal supplies heat even after the burning is done, but with self-burning incense it burns and goes out. Either scrape the material off the charcoal or remove it from the heat once it has burned.

Magickal Considerations

When making incense for use in ritual, or for any magickal purpose, you also have to consider the magick properties of any of the ingredients you use in your incense. It complicates your task as an incense maker, but it also makes your rewards much greater. I'll discuss that in more detail later.

Aromatics generally fall into one of three categories: resins, plant materials, or woods. There are some aromatics that won't fit into these categories, but most will. Each individual type of aromatic will behave a little differently in your incense, so it's important to understand the differences.

Resins

Resins are the dried sap or fluid from plants and, more often, trees. Frankincense, myrrh, and dragon's blood are all resins. Resins are often sticky (more so when heated), so use care when grinding them. If you overheat them inside your grinder you'll have a tough time cleaning them out afterward. Most resins can be ground to a powder fairly easily, although some retain enough moisture that they can get messy (this is especially true of myrrh). Resins are usually very powerful. As a result, they should be used sparingly. When using a resin for the first time or when experimenting with one, use caution and only add a small amount to your blend. On many occasions I've been able to cut the amount of resin in a recipe in half without harming its scent at all, so don't underestimate their strength.

Plant Materials

Although most aromatics are taken from plants, by this category I refer specifically to leaf, stem, or root material. Wood is in a category all its own, but plant materials would include the roots, bark, or the leaves of trees. Patchouli, sage, lavender, and many other aromatics are plant materials. Most plant materials are easy to powder. Their burning properties range from eager-to-burn to very difficult. Most of the items you grow yourself for incense making will fall into this category. Sadly, the vast majority of the plant matter in the world smells very much the same when burning. Luckily for us, there are hundreds of plants that work very well and produce great scents. Just don't be too disappointed when the wonderful smelling flowers you grew this summer turn out to smell like a wet dog when your incense is burned. That's why it's so important to test a new aromatic before rolling it into incense.

Woods

This final category of aromatics refers to very fragrant woods. Sandalwood, pine, and cedar are all examples of fragrant wood. Woods are, not surprisingly, the easiest aromatics to burn. If you have any trouble burning a wood, then it probably has some moisture trapped in it and should be carefully dried before using it again. Woods are generally the hardest aromatic to powder and should be purchased in powdered form when possible. As long as the wood has a strong fragrance, it can be used as an aromatic. If a wood has a weak scent, then it can be used as a base.

Bases

A base material is usually wood powder. Many types of wood can be used, but in general I get better results from soft woods rather than hard woods. The key to a good base wood powder is scent. You want as little scent as possible and the scent there is needs to be pleasant. A base material with a strong scent can be used (such as pine), but you then have to think about it not only as a base but as an aromatic as well. You wouldn't want to use pine as a base if you were trying to create a floral scent for example.

This is a time where you can actually get the best results from inexpensive materials. If you wanted to use cedar as an aromatic, you'd want to use wood with a high quantity of natural oil. On the other hand, if you use cedar as a base then the less oil it has the less scent it will add to your incense mixtures. Highly processed wood powder (such as wood that has had its oil extracted) often offers the best base material. Red cedar (which isn't a cedar at all) has little scent and is a good base material, although it is difficult to powder.

Base materials serve two basic purposes. The first is to improve the burning properties of the incense. Many aromatics are reluctant to burn and the base aids in the burning process. Leafy plant materials in particular can be very hard to burn. The base material that you use can improve the burning qualities of your incense overall. One of the first ways to improve the burning properties of an incense mixture is to increase the amount of base material. Although it is not a wood, clove is also an important base material. Adding clove to an incense blend causes it to burn hotter and thus helps you use aromatics that are harder to burn.

The second purpose of a base material is to improve its scent. It does this by "mellowing" the scent, or "muting" it. If your aromatic blend produces too strong a scent when burned, increasing the amount of base material will help a great deal. It's like "turning down the volume" on the scent. Because of this you should use the least amount of base possible that still produces a blend that burns and smells good. Adding too much base will make incense that burns well but doesn't have the desired power.

Binders

The final component of rolled incense is the binder. The binder serves as the glue that holds your incense together and allows you to shape and form the incense as you please. Binders range from plant gums to (according to popular legend anyway) animal dung. For this book I'll focus on easy to use binders that can be reasonably easily located. I say "reasonably easily" because finding a binder may be your most difficult task. I'll discuss locating binders in detail in chapter 4.

Gum Arabic or Acacia

You'll see this as a recommended binder in many "traditional" recipes as well as many new ones. It was one of the first incense binders used in the West and I think it should be left in the past. But it is a little easier to find than many of the other binders so it deserves some discussion. Gum arabic (or gum acacia) is a white powder sometimes with a mild minty smell. When mixed with water it forms a glue. It is often used to thicken sauces and soda pop. Although I know that most of the publicly available information on incense making uses gum arabic as a binder I truly can't recommend it.

As an incense binder it will hold your incense together but it has some drawbacks. First, it is very sticky. That makes it hard to handle since it tends to stick to your hands and your tools. It can also crystallize on the surface of your incense and in extreme cases even flake off. In general, it's tough to work with and I don't recommend it for beginning incense makers. It isn't well suited for molding or extruding. On the positive side, you can sometimes find acacia powder not only in herb shops but also in the spice section of gourmet shops. If you find a recipe that calls for gum arabic I'd recommend you replace it with one of the other binders listed in this book.

Gum Tragacanth

Gum tragacanth is used in the food industry to thicken soups and gravy. It's also used to make pills and icing for baked goods. A great deal of the colorful icing you see in the bakery is sugar, water, and gum tragacanth. It is also an excellent binder for incense. It is a light-tan to cream-colored powder. It has a very mild scent that is reminiscent of sweetened flour. It is strong and pliable. It's also fairly forgiving for the novice incense maker. It works well for hand rolling, molding, and extruding.

Guar Gum

Guar gum is very similar to tragacanth. It is a white powder with virtually no scent. It is also used in making food and pharmaceuticals. As a binder it also works well for rolling, molding and extruding. The price is also very similar to tragacanth, although guar gum is often a bit cheaper. You can usually substitute guar gum for an equal amount of tragacanth or vice versa.

Makko

This is hardly a new binder. Japanese masters have used it for a thousand years, but it is fairly new on the Western market. Also known as "tabu," it is a light-brown powder of medium coarseness. It is the bark of a tree (*Machillus thunbergii*) and it's simply an amazing material. It is a nice binder, although it is also a sticky one. It isn't as strong as gum binders, but its benefits far outweigh that shortcoming. It not only has very little scent of its own, it also has a wonderful capacity to absorb the scents around it. When mixed with your aromatics it easily takes on their scent. Because of this, it is important to keep your makko in a sealed container and away from any aromatics with a strong scent because it will absorb the smell. It isn't perfectly suited for molding, although mixed properly it can work. It is excellent for extruding.

The best aspect of using makko is that it is not only a binder, it is also an excellent base material! It improves the burning properties of any incense blend. Some people call it a "burning agent" because it so greatly improves the burning properties of any blend. You can use it in place of any other base or you can use it in addition to other base materials if you wish. You'll find that its wonderful properties will make it worth seeking out. You'll also have no doubt as to why Japanese incense masters have used it for a thousand years.

Honey

Honey isn't an acceptable binder for self-burning incense, but it is used as a binder in many "moist" incense recipes. Anyone who has ever handled honey knows it is very sticky. Thus it does a great job of binding moist incense. Just remember that incense made with a honey binder has to be burned over a heat source (like charcoal) and isn't self-burning.

A final note about binders. Binders can vary widely in strength. For example, tragacanth is sold in the food industry in five different grades, ranging from weak to strong. Odds are that you will never receive this information when you buy the binder. It is unlikely that even your supplier will know which grade the binder is. You may need to adjust the amount of binder in any given recipe depending on the strength of the binder you have. Use the least amount of binder you can to get the incense to hold together properly. Too much binder can actually keep your incense from burning. Too little binder can cause cracking and brittleness.

Liquids

Your binder doesn't go to work until you add water to it. The water activates the binder and glues your incense together. You don't have to limit yourself to only using water. Just carefully consider before using other liquids.

Water

Water is always a good choice. For best results, use distilled water. The chemicals and minerals in your tap water might have an impact on your incense, although tap water will work just fine if that's all you have. Tap water should be allowed to sit for an hour or two to allow the chlorine to dissipate. Water shouldn't modify the scent of your incense at all. For magickal incense you might want to use water blessed in a magick circle or water that you've collected from a place sacred to you.

Wine

I've made a lot of fine incense with white wine. Does it make a difference in the scent? Well, not really that I've noticed. Using a highly fragrant wine might impart a new scent to your incense. Wine is also a common component in incense made for ritual use.

Soy Sauce

I've seen some recipes that use soy sauce. I've experimented with it and didn't find it to be to my taste. It is mostly water, so you can certainly use it. Try it yourself and you might find that you love the effect.

Alcohol

You can use alcohol, but I don't recommend it. A lot of commercial incense is made using alcohol to "extend" the fragrance oils they use. It certainly has an effect on the scent. If you do use alcohol, keep in mind that the higher the alcohol content, the less water it has. So you'd want to avoid anything over 80 proof (that's 40 percent alcohol by volume). I don't know why you'd want to, but you could. You might get interesting results from using low-proof schnapps of various flavors. This wouldn't be something that I'd favor in magickal incense, but if you do then by all means use it.

Honey

Honey can be used in incense making (as seen in the last section), but it isn't well suited for the "liquids" category. Most honey is only 20 percent water, so it isn't a good choice to activate binders. You can certainly add honey to your rolled incense, just be sure to include a proper liquid with it to activate the binder. That can be as simple as mixing the honey in a 1:3 ratio with water (1 teaspoon of honey for every 3 teaspoon of water).

Other Liquids

You can use virtually any liquid that is mostly water. Fruit juice, soft drinks, coffee, tea, or anything else that is primarily water will work. The only drawback is that most of those liquids will make your incense stink. Sugar doesn't smell good when burned, so avoid sugary liquids. Don't try to use oil to activate your binder. Oils don't contain any significant amounts of water and won't work. Experiment with different liquids if the mood strikes you, but you'll get wonderful results from water every time. If there is any type of herbal brew that you use in your rituals you might want to use that as your liquid for magickal incense.

Temperature

It might not seem important at first thought, but the temperature of your liquid can have a big effect on the incense making process. It's critical to remember the dangers of handling hot water. Speaking as one who has had a severe burn from water, hot water needs to be handled with care. Never let children handle hot water.

The advantages of using hot water might be worth the discomforts. Hot water generally makes your incense softer, easier to handle, and much easier to extrude. The second major advantage is in drying time. Spaghetti sticks rolled using hot water are often dry in less than twelve hours. Using hot water is the only good technique to hurry the drying process (although that quick drying will cause the sticks to warp extensively). A final benefit to using hot water arises if you accidentally add too much water to your blend. Too much water can make it impossible to shape the incense. If you've used hot water, you can cool the overly wet mixture and it will be much more shapable.

On the other hand, incense made with cold water also has its advantages. First, it is more comfortable to handle and you don't have the dangers of handling hot water. Cold water will also slow the drying time of your incense. While you might think that's a bad thing, it is actually much better to dry your incense slowly as you'll see later. The fact that it dries slower also gives you more time to work with the incense dough before it dries out.

Different binders also act differently with changes in water temperature. Makko, for example, prefers water at room temperature or colder. Guar gum is usually easier to handle and extrude when made with warm or hot water. You might want to experiment to find the best temperature for your binder, but if you are unsure then use room-temperature water.

The Science of Incense

Now, I'm no scientist but science definitely plays an important role in incense. Physics in particular is important. There is a basic physical problem that has to be overcome with any incense that you make: plant matter doesn't always want to burn. This is the first hurdle the incense maker has to overcome. I discussed the importance of the shape of your incense in the last chapter, but it bears repeating. Make sure that in any batch of incense you make with a new recipe, make at least a few thin, spaghetti-sized sticks of incense. Test those first when your incense is completely dry. If your spaghetti sticks of incense won't burn then you will have to reformulate the recipe. If the spaghetti sticks burn but larger sticks or cones won't burn, you might want to reformulate the recipe or just be happy to burn the spaghetti sticks.

Another important aspect of the science of incense making is avoiding dangerous materials. Science and tradition have identified many problem materials. You should never add anything poisonous to your incense. American mistletoe, for example, although called for in some recipes, should be avoided or used with extreme care in incense. Materials such as saltpeter are also known to give off potentially dangerous fumes and should likewise be avoided.

In a related area, science has also shown us that burning some substances can have a significant effect on brain chemistry. Just as smoking tobacco or cannabis has a significant effect upon people, so does burning such substances in our incense. In fact, this is one of the basic purposes of incense. It certainly isn't the same profound effect that smoking has, but if you are concerned with remaining free of mind-altering substances then you need to be careful what materials you put in your incense. Damiana, skullcap, wild lettuce, frankincense, and others are known to alter people's state of mind. In fact, many people use incense as an aid to meditation with just this fact in mind. Some incense is formulated to aid the brain during meditation through chemistry.

The Art of Incense

Although there is a fair amount of science involved in incense burning, incense making is at least as much art as science. I often call incense "combustible art." It is that in a couple of aspects. First is the art of the blend—the aromatic art. Finding a blend that doesn't smell bad is often a new incense maker's first good result. Creating a blend that smells nice is a wonderful experience and you will continue to make that first good recipe again and again. But when you create a great scent it is truly art. We're used to seeing art or listening to it. But to smell it is rare. Only incense, nature, and good cooks play well in the scent arena. It's an overlooked sense for the arts, but it's at least as important as any of the others.

Incense can also be art in its form. Incense dough is a wonderful medium for an artist to use. It does tend to develop some deformations during the drying process, but aside from that it is fun and very flexible. From coils to hand-rolled cones, simple basic incense is beautiful to look at and touch as well as smell. You can also get quite creative. From simple things like writing in incense to complex impressionistic shapes, the incense clay will offer you lots of opportunity to express yourself with form. Look in your local hobby or toy shop for tools meant for working clay. They will serve you wonderfully and open up your creative abilities. If you design your art properly, it will also be a display to be burned and to offer entertainment to the eye while it pleases the nose.

The Magick of Incense

Incense used for magick is always strongest when properly empowered. By making the incense yourself, or at least being involved in each step, you can assure that the incense is totally empowered for your purposes and that no stray, outside influences have affected it. In addition to the intentional empowering that you do as you make the incense, you also passively empower it simply by the process of mixing, blending, and kneading. The fact that your hands shaped the incense and it was squeezed between your fingers while still wet is an empowering act. It is an intimate involvement with incense that you couldn't possibly get from incense made by someone else.

Magick is also key when selecting the components for your incense. Components you've grown or collected are powerful elements in your incense. By making your own you're also able to avoid components that might pose karmic or ethical concerns. Who knows what's in the incense you've been buying? Any incense might work for mundane purposes, but when it comes to the incense you use in ritual you can never surpass the power of incense you've made or helped make.

Incense composition is more than just a combination of aromatics, bases, and binders. It is also an expression of the incense maker and her use of the tools and materials available to her. Proper combination of materials is the start of the process, then the chance for physical art begins. Considering the amount of aromatics available, you can make a nearly endless variety of works of art for the nose. You can look at how to combine ingredients from many perspectives, but I think that this model is perfect for the home incense maker.

Chapter Three

How to Use Incense

Understanding how to use incense is obviously valuable knowledge for the maker of incense. Even if you never make incense yourself (which would be a true shame), this is important information for everyone who uses incense. Before making your first batch of incense, at least skim over this chapter. Which form of incense you choose to make could be heavily influenced by how it is burned.

Incense Burners

An incense burner can be as simple as an old can or as elaborate as an ornate temple burner. Some incense users are content to own one or two simple burners. Others have giant collections of burners from around the world. It's important to buy the right burner for the type of incense that you make, especially for safety.

Cones and Cylinders

Choosing a good cone burner is important. While nearly anything can catch the ash from a stick, a cone or a spaghetti stick will burn completely. That means anything you use as a burner for cones, cylinders, or spaghetti sticks has to be able to withstand the heat. Never burn cones on wood.

The most common form of cone burner is the small brass burner. It is a raised brass "bowl" with a lid. Brass burners of this style are wonderfully functional and will last forever if you buy a good one and take care of it.

Don't buy a burner that's too small. If you only see one size at a store, then you probably need to find a different store. A good brass burner should have a mouth at least an inch and a half across (two to three inches is best). If you can't put three fingers in the mouth at once, it's too small. It is best to light cones and then put them in the burner. If the mouth is too small you'll burn your fingers. Ideally, the walls of the "dish" should be at least one inch tall. This is to make sure the cones can't fall out.

A note about lids. I've heard many complaints about cone burners that "put the cone out" when the lid is put on. If you buy a larger burner that is properly ventilated, cones will burn with the lid on. You'll have to clean the lid frequently to keep oils and resins from ruining the finish if that's important to you. Over time, the lid will take on a fragrance all its own. That scent will be released when the lid is heated, so it will become a part of any incense you burn. Some burners can become nicely "seasoned" in this way over time. If your incense burner extinguishes your cones, you need to buy a larger one.

It's a very good idea to put a small amount of sand or ash at the bottom of cone burners. This will improve the air flow under the cone (to help make the entire cone burn) and help to protect your burner. You should replace sand after every four or five uses. If you use ash it can be sifted and re-used indefinitely. Never use a brass burner on a wooden surface. Brass conducts heat pretty well, and even raised burners can burn the wood they sit on. A ceramic tile or ashtray works fine.

For the serious burner of cones, I recommend soapstone burners. Most forms of burner and ash catcher are available in soapstone and they are the best for cone burning. You'll usually pay a little more for the soapstone, but it is well worth a few cents. Most soapstone cone burners can be used on a wooden surface (don't chance it with a new burner, use it on tile or in an ash tray the first time and see how hot it gets before using it on wood). Ash or sand in the bottom is still an excellent idea.

Loose Incense

You basically need a tiny charcoal grill. Often they are made of brass . They can be mere overgrown cone burners. They are large brass bowls (some with lids). The mouth of your burner should be at least three and a half inches across (four to five is better). You can either put sand or ash in the bottom or use a piece of metal screen that is bent around the edges to let it stand an inch or so off the bed of sand. That way you can scrape ashes from the top of your charcoal into the bottom before adding new items to burn.

Put one or two charcoal bricks (only side by side, never stacked) in your burner on top of the wire mesh or sand. Light the edges of the bricks with a match or barbecue lighter (bamboo charcoal, which is preferred, may require an extra effort to light) and you're ready to go. Be sure not to touch the sides of the censer when in use. It is very hot! Never use a censer on wood.

Sticks (with Bamboo Rods)

The most common stick holder is known as a "boat." These are long, flat wooden pieces that curve at one end. There is a small hole in the raised end and the uncoated end of the bamboo stick is inserted through the hole. This is the most basic form of ash catcher. You'll find these virtually anywhere that sells incense. They are also made of bone, ceramic, glass, and stone. Some have an enclosed box beneath the curved piece. That is supposed to be a storage area for unburned sticks, but I wouldn't keep incense in a wooden box unless the sticks were bagged in plastic or similarly sealed. Many of these catchers are inlaid with brass or hand painted. It's also nice to buy a cheap plain one and paint it yourself.

There is another category of stick holders that I call "trees." These holders are usually wooden or stone centerpieces with a series of holes drilled into the top. They will hold several sticks at once and hold the sticks nearly straight up and down. They require less space and hold more incense than boats, so they are a good investment.

Sticks (not spaghetti sticks, however) can also be inserted into the ground. Push the uncoated end of the bamboo into dry ground, clear away any combustible materials from underneath the stick, and light it up. Take care not to burn incense outdoors if the wind is strong as it might blow sparks off the end that could start a fire. Also keep burning incense away from paths where anyone might walk next to them.

Spaghetti Sticks

Spaghetti sticks, cylinders, and cones burn completely so they can't be used in wooden incense boats. They are usually safe to use in soapstone or metal boats. The best way to burn spaghetti sticks is in a censer. Light one end and insert the other end into the ash far enough to allow the stick to stand straight. This type of incense and burner together is usually the least messy of any combination.

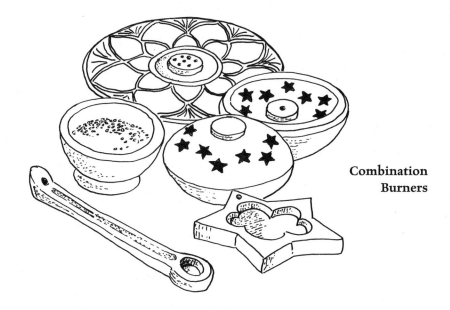

26

Combination Burners

Various Censers

Combination Burners

Some manufacturers make burners that can handle several types of incense. Usually they are made from soapstone or are ceramic. Most are large cone-burning dishes with special lids or holes drilled in the bottom for sticks. Cylinders and even loose incense can be burned in ones with a large enough mouth. Spaghetti sticks can also be used in them. Sand or ash is also a great idea in the bottom of your combination burner, as long as it doesn't block any of the holes or other special features.

Censers

The censer is the best type of burner for anyone serious about incense and is the typical incense burner used in rituals. It's also the ultimate type of combination burner. A censer is a dish, bowl, ashtray, or similar object filled with a nonflammable substance, most often sand or ash but gravel, decorative rock, etc., can also be used. Sticks, cylinders, and spaghetti sticks can be inserted into the sand or ash. Cones, coils, and charcoal for loose incense can be burned on the surface of the ash (coils will usually put themselves out when burned on the surface of sand). They can also be used for kodo-style or makko burning. A good censer will handle all of your incense burner needs.

Lighting Incense

To light stick, cone, or cylinder incense, hold a lit match or, better yet, a butane lighter, to the tapered or coated end of the incense (or either end of a spaghetti stick or cylinder). Hold the flame there for ten seconds (more for some) then take the flame away. If everything is perfect, the incense will continue to flame for a second or two and then the flame will go out and the end will continue to glow and slowly burn. Some incense will not go out on its own. If it flames for more than twenty seconds, blow the flame out.

The smell you get just after the flame goes out is not necessarily the way the incense really smells. Incense is made up of materials that will burn at different rates while flaming, so all you smell in that first few seconds are the materials that didn't vanish in the flame. Give it twenty or thirty seconds, then the true scent will start to come through.

When it comes to dipped incense (as most commercial incense is), you might even notice that long after the incense is lit there are long wisps of black smoke in the air. If you reach up and touch one you'll discover that it's not smoke at all. It is actually a long chain of oil molecules. They use such high quantities of synthetic oil that it doesn't all burn so these chains of oil are also spewed into the air. One of the most popular brands of incense in the United States is notorious for doing this. That's one of the reasons I recommend sticking with natural incense instead of that synthetic stuff. Remember, your incense should give off a pale white smoke, that's the sign of good combustion. If your incense gives off black smoke, that means that it's not burning completely and needs to be reformulated (reducing the amount of oil in a recipe usually helps).

As you make incense, you might roll cones (or other shapes) that won't burn. This is also a problem with commercial cones, both rolled and dipped. Although I will discuss this in-depth in chapter 9, I wanted to mention a clever little trick when you encounter this problem. Try burning the cone upside down. Try it—it really works. Read chapter 9 for other ideas.

28

Hazards

There are a number of factors you need to keep in mind when it comes to safety. First is fire safety. Since incense must be burned you should always be conscious of where it is and what it might come into contact with. Here are some important fire safety guidelines.

1. Make certain that no part of burning incense comes into contact with wood or other flammable materials.

2. Never burn incense inside cupboards or with anything hanging above the burning incense. The rising heat from the incense (along with the smoke) can cause discolorations and is potentially a fire hazard. If you want to use incense smoke to scent clothing, hang it at least eighteen inches above the burning incense.

3. Incense burners can heat up. Even soapstone burners get hot. Always be careful where you place the burner. A hot burner can damage or discolor wooden surfaces. They can also burn you if you try to move them while they are in use unless they have a chain or a handle.

4. Never leave burning incense unattended. If you have to leave while your incense is still burning, put it out. If you have to, you can put it out under water. A better method, if you use a censer, is to turn the incense upside down and bury the burning end in the sand or ash. That will put it out but still allow you to relight it at some future time. To put out a coil of incense you can break off the glowing tip and discard it in water.

5. Although this seems obvious to say, burning incense is hot. Just grazing the glowing tip of burning incense can cause a significant burn on skin and clothing. It really smarts!

6. Watch burning incense and make certain the ash is dropping where it should. If the ash is falling outside its container you might need to reposition it or use a different burner. It's a very good idea to contain the ash. It can discolor furniture and might even be hot enough to be a fire hazard itself.

7. Remember that the sign of Fire is powerful and deserves your reverence. Do not be careless with burning incense or charcoal out of respect for the power of Fire.

Another important consideration with incense and safety is the material that you burn. Burning loose incense over charcoal may pose a hazard according to some experts. I personally have never noticed a problem, but some have suggested that burning charcoal in a well-insulated, poorly ventilated, or enclosed environment may cause dangerous levels of carbon monoxide to collect. This is especially true when you are using the "self-lighting" type of charcoal or incense that contains saltpeter, but even the finest charcoal might have this effect. As I said, I've never encountered a problem myself but it's best to be careful.

You can buy one very good incense burner and it will last your entire life. Or, if you prefer, you can collect them and own hundreds. Just keep in mind which type of incense can be used in which type of burners and where to place them for safety. If used with care, incense is quite safe and amazingly pleasant.

Incense for Magickal Use

Although most practitioners of ritual magick know about using incense on their altars, don't ever limit yourself to that one use. Incense is also perfect for the time before your rituals. Do you enjoy a cleansing bath before your rituals? That's another perfect time to enjoy your incense art. Some people like to burn a nice cleansing incense during this process. Others prefer to burn the same incense that they will use during their rituals so as to shift their mindset to the forthcoming spell work. Experiment and discover what type of incense you like during this preparation stage and you'll further the value of your art.

Incense is also a perfect tool to help create sacred space. If you're like me, you don't have the space to devote an entire room to ritual use. In that case, it is paramount to differentiate between space normally used for mundane purposes (such as your bedroom) and the same space being used for ritual. Cleaning is the most basic way to do that. Setting up an altar and tools is another. But nothing imparts the fact that the space is now being used for sacred purposes than the impact of incense. I like to use a cleansing scent like copal to prepare my sacred spaces, but you should use the incense you've made for that purpose.

Incense is an excellent tool for use during any spell work. Not only can it be used for cleansing, it can also be used to energize your ritual space. The amazing scent of aloeswood, for example, can palpably raise the energy level in a room. Incense is also a wonderful offering to invite specific spirits or deities into your circle or sacred space. That is the most basic use of incense. It is an offering that brings joy to you as well as the spirits. Incense is also a great tool for banishment. Using incense made for this purpose can provide an instant effect in banishment rituals. Specific incense can be made for any spell work you plan to do and you'll be amazed at how it enhances your work.

Practitioners who commonly use loose incense and charcoal in their rituals are very familiar with using different aromatics or blends during different spells (or different parts of a single spell), but users of self-combustible incense usually just light up a stick at the start of the ritual and then let it burn out. You don't have to be limited in that way. If you make spaghetti sticks or cylinders, they can be easily cut to any length and thus used just as different aromatics are used in loose incense. You could have a short stick of cinnamon, a long stick of lavender, and a short stick of sage. When one burns out, light the next one from an appropriate candle on your altar. This is a safer and easier alternative to using charcoal and loose incense.

You can actually "program" the timing of your rituals or spell work. Use incense as a timing device. When one stick burns out, you know it's time to move to the next stage of your ritual. Once you become practiced at making incense you can even learn to make one long coil with different types of incense. That way you need only light the one coil and as the scent changes it acts like a clock for your spell work. Detailed examples of using incense on your altar or in your rituals can be found in Appendix D.

Never limit yourself. You can use your incense making skills to enhance your spiritual life in many ways. Use incense creatively not only in ritual, but before and after it as well. It is also a perfect type of "little magick" all by itself. Just lighting the right stick of incense at the right moment can totally change the energy of your day.

Chapter Four

Selecting Materials

Just as a cake is only as good as its ingredients, the scent your incense gives is directly dependent upon the materials you use to make it. For new incense makers, just finding ingredients can be challenging. But as time goes by you'll begin to seek out higher quality materials. Whether you're buying over the Internet or in person, growing or gathering materials, you need to know the basics of choosing incense ingredients.

Purchasing Aromatics

Most incense makers purchase their ingredients. You'll find that buying incense ingredients is very much like buying food. You can buy the finest meats, cheeses, and oils to prepare a gourmet meal. Similarly, you can make incense from ingredients that cost more than gold from the far corners of the world. On the other hand you can make a perfectly wonderful meal from a bit of potato, butter, salt, and pepper. Likewise, you can make very nice incense using materials from your local area or that are quite inexpensive.

The first factor is your budget. This is an important consideration for most people. How much do you want to spend? Some aloeswood costs hundreds of dollars per ounce, but who can afford that? Whenever planning a new incense recipe, consider the cost of the materials. Personally,

I enjoy incense enough that I don't mind spending a little extra money to get a higher quality product, but very nice incense can be created on a budget.

A second key factor in choosing ingredients is selection. Just like when buying produce, it is important to select ingredients that are of good quality. The most important aspect of that is choosing suppliers who are reputable. If someone has a hundred different aromatics for sale and they all cost the same amount of money per ounce, that is not a reputable seller. The price of sage, for example, is far lower than dragon's blood. Anyone selling them for the same price is unlikely to be selling real dragon's blood resin. Oftentimes these substances are merely wood powder with some synthetic oil added to them for scent.

It also important to inspect your incense ingredients. Whether powdered or in whole form, they should be dry and free from any mold or mildew. There also shouldn't be a lot of foreign matter (wood chips, rocks, etc.) mixed in with the aromatic. Some unscrupulous sellers will add that sort of material in order to save money (for themselves of course). As with food, it's important to become familiar with what you are buying. Before investing a lot of money in a "high-quality" ingredient, do some reading and make certain that you are getting what you pay for. A high price is not a promise of high quality.

A final aspect to quality is the ethical quality of the material. Animal products, poached materials and other ethical considerations are important. For a more detailed discussion of this topic, please see Appendix C.

Perhaps the best advice when it comes to selecting materials is to stick with reputable merchants. The vast majority of people who sell incense making supplies aren't in the business in order to get rich. Most are people who love incense and will do all they can to help you locate the finest materials. Sadly, there are exceptions to this. Although I have been in this business for many years, I have only dealt with a handful of sellers who weren't as honest as they should have been. They are rare, but there are a few tips for spotting them. First is looking for those who sell a wide assortment of aromatics at the same price (as discussed earlier) or who add foreign objects to their aromatics. Another way for detecting fraud is by testing the aromatics. Often times, adulterated powders will smell nice until they are burned. If you find a sweet-smelling sandalwood powder that stinks when burned, it is most likely not the real thing. One way to avoid this problem entirely is to buy materials in their whole form. It is much harder to create a fake chunk of dragon's blood resin than to fake a red powder that smells like dragon's blood. The odds are that you'll only buy from a bad vendor once. As soon as you see that the material is suspect you'll know not to buy from them again. A final tip for avoiding fraud is to never buy extremely expensive materials. Fraud is far more common with the very rare and expensive materials. See Appendix C for a more detailed discussion of this problem.

Buying Binders

Binders are often the most difficult ingredients for new incense makers to locate, so I wanted to discuss them separately. Although gum arabic is the easiest binder to find, I would urge you to look a little harder and find a better binder. Makko is fairly new to the American market, so try to locate a local supplier if you can. If you live in a major city, you might be able to find all the binders listed in this book locally. Even if you don't live in one of those cities, you can still find some of the binders.

The best first step is to grab your local phone book. First check "herbs" and see if your town has an herb store. Be sure you call them and check, as many times the businesses listed under "herbs" only sell capsules of herbs for use in health care. Next, look under "cake decorating supplies" (or any similar category). Many cake decoration suppliers sell guar gum or gum tragacanth. You might try your local hobby shop as well. Some hobby shops have a cake decorating section where you might find gum powders. If you can't locate a supplier that way, look under "chemicals." Most chemical suppliers stock or can special order both guar gum and tragacanth. You will usually pay top-dollar when purchasing this way, but you usually get the highest-quality material as well. If you're using binders purchased from a chemical supplier, use care when making incense with them. They tend to be the strongest grade so you might need to reduce the amount of binder in your recipes. Overbinding can keep your incense from burning.

If you can't locate any binders where you live, you can turn to the Internet. To those of you who don't have access to the Internet, most of the suppliers listed in this book also accept orders through the mail. But hopefully you can go to your local library or community center so that you can visit these websites. Even if you choose to make payment through the mail, visiting the website allows you to see new products, hints and tips, availability, and much more. Incense suppliers generally love incense and will talk your ear off about the subject if you ask them a question! Both as a practical matter and to help minimize problems and fraud, I think you should buy from suppliers in your own country whenever possible.

A list of Internet suppliers appears on my website listed in Appendix B, but there are always more and more websites being added every month. Go to your favorite search engine and type in "incense making supplies" or something similar and you should get a great list of places to look. It's also a good idea to check the Internet for any specific ingredient you might need. Doing a search on "makko," for example, might not only yield the names of some new vendors selling makko, it might also point you to web pages where you might learn new ways to use makko or recipes that contain it.

Growing Incense Materials

Many crafty people are avid gardeners. Incense making offers you another wonderful outlet to use the plants that you grow. Although garden plants are most often used as aromatics, you can grow plants useful in other ways as well. Best of all, once made into incense your garden plants can bring you joy long after the garden is gone. Whether growing or collecting materials, carefully wash all plant materials before you bring them indoors for drying. Shake as much water from the plants as possible and towel dry them if necessary. Avoid using material that has been recently sprayed with insecticide or other chemical products. This is especially true for material used in magickal incense.

Selecting Plants

Just as in nature, the bulk of garden plants aren't properly aromatic for use in incense making. In general, flowers from your garden won't be of much use. Sadly, even fragrant flowers often have little smell, or smell unpleasant, when burned. Thankfully, there are some notable exceptions. Fragrant jasmine, honeysuckle, and lavender are all flowers that can work very well in your incense. Of course, different cultivars (different varieties of the same plant species) will yield different results so you always need to test your dried flowers on charcoal. I've never found a lavender flower that didn't work well in incense, but it is possible that some cultivars I've never used might not smell good. That's one of the reasons you need to test your aromatics before adding them to your incense.

In addition to flowers, many other items from the garden can be used in incense making. Your herb garden in particular will be very useful. Sage, oregano, cilantro, basil, and many other herb leaves are perfect for incense making. You'll also find seeds, such as coriander (the seeds from your cilantro plants), cucumber, dill, and others to be great for your incense.

In addition to using plants from the garden as aromatics, you can find other uses as well. I was once contacted by someone who wanted to roll incense onto a lavender flower stem. I didn't understand why until they told me that lavender stores the bulk of its oil in the stems rather than the flowers or leaves. This is a much better approach than using a bamboo rod, although you need to expect it to be aromatic, so it wouldn't work with all scents. You can also find base materials in your garden. While you're testing the seeds, flowers, and leaves from your garden, test the plants stems as well.

Occasionally, you will find one whose stems or stalks have very little scent (usually from the poorer plants in your garden). If you find one with little scent when burned, powder a small amount of it. Make a small pile of the powder in your censer and light it at the top. If it smolders and burns completely (or nearly completely) it might serve well as a base. More often you'll find that the stems will have a scent similar to, although less pronounced than, the leaves. If the stems burn well and their scent complements the aromatic parts of a plant, try them as a base material.

Drying Materials

Before you can put those plants from your garden (or materials collected in the wild) to use, you must properly prepare them. Understanding the steps to preparation is also important if you store your ingredients in their whole form. There are two steps to this process. The first step, drying, is simple and straightforward. The second step, powdering, is a little trickier.

It is critical to dry all of your plant materials completely. The only incense components that don't have to be completely dry are resins, and if they are not dry they need to be processed correctly in order to burn. There are several techniques for drying plant materials and any of them will work fine. You should, however, take care not to try to rush the drying process.

- Never dry plant materials in direct sunlight. Sunlight can cause chemical changes in the material as well as discoloring it and drying out the desired oils.

- Never dry plant material in an oven or near a heater. It's tempting to hurry the drying process this way, but it is much better to allow the process to take whatever time it needs to minimize the loss of valuable oils.

Bag Drying

This is a good technique for drying material that can be bundled such as material on stems, large root parts, or evergreen needles. You can bundle the material together using a string or thread. Avoid using rubber bands as they can break before the drying process ends and your bundle will fall apart. Using only one bundle per bag, insert a bundle into a paper bag large enough that the stems don't touch the sides. Close the top of the bag around the base of the stems and tie it closed with a long piece of string. You can then hang the bag using this piece of string. Pick a location that doesn't have high humidity and that avoids direct exposure to sunlight (or large amounts of artificial light). If you don't have a location to hang the bags, you can dry them flat although I really don't recommend it. Be certain to rotate the bags a quarter turn every few days if you can't hang them.

There are a couple of advantages to using the bag method. One advantage is the protection that the bag offers. It helps shield the plant material from light and helps keep it free from dust and insects as it dries. Should any flowers or leaves come loose during the drying process, the bag is there to catch them.

Another advantage is ease of handling and labeling. You should write the name of the material and any special details (where purchased or harvested, when collected, etc.). This is important because different dried plants materials can often look the same. Without those labels you might forget which plant is which. You might also find that the same species of plant harvested from different places can have different scents. Labeling is the only way to track that information.

Screen Drying

Bag drying is great if you can do it, but it isn't well suited for drying large amounts of material or for drying materials like individual leaves or wood. Wood should be chopped into small pieces or shaved into thin pieces if being used as base. If wood is to be used as an aromatic it should be left in chunks, as large as you can easily handle and store, until just before use.

You can use many materials for a screen. Something as large as chicken wire or as fine as panty hose can be used. I use a simple one-inch-wide wooden frame that is about five feet long and one foot wide with "contractor's fabric" (a metal screen with $1/4$-inch holes) stapled to it. You can make a simple screen by using a wire coat hanger. Straighten out the hook of the hanger and use it as a handle. Reshape the looped part of the hanger into a circle. You can then stretch out an old pair of nylon hose over the loop and staple it around the edges. You can even use a screen door laid over a pair of sawhorses. Anything that will allow air to circulate completely around the plant material. With large leaves you can even use a baker's cooling rack.

When using a screen to dry, be certain that each individual piece of material (each leaf, plant, etc.) is isolated. Don't let different bits touch because that will slow the drying process.

Put only a single layer on the screen and make certain that there is good air-flow all around the screen. Also, don't try to use a fan while screen drying since your plants might blow away as they dry.

Screen drying is the only way to deal with a lot of plant material, including large leaves or wood. You can also construct many different screens and use them all in a relatively small area by stacking them. So if you really want to harvest a lot of material from your garden you'll need to devote some space to screens for drying. Most plant materials will dry completely in a few weeks, you won't need to leave your screens up all year.

You might be tempted to use a food dehydrator or something similar to speed up the drying of your plant materials. Don't give in to temptation! Rapid drying of plant materials can cause them to lose their important oils. No matter which drying method you choose, let nature take its course and allow the drying to take place in its own time.

Powdering

This is a critical step for incense making, although "powdering" isn't a perfect term. Although powdered materials burn the best, many materials you use will really be very finely chopped rather than truly powdered. If you grind your plant materials with a mortar and pestle or a mill, then the material you get will be powdered. If, on the other hand, you use a coffee grinder or a blender, you are actually chopping the material rather than powdering it. Although you can chop it quite finely, it will never be as fine as a powder. Some incense makers feel that chopped materials preserve more of their natural oils and prefer not to powder any ingredients if it can be avoided.

Mortar and Pestle

This is a good basic tool for all incense makers. Often, especially when working with resins, powdering begins with the mortar and pestle. Large chunks of material need to be broken into small pieces before processing them further and the mortar and pestle is a great way to do that. You can continue to powder using the mortar and pestle if you wish. You can use the pestle first to

Mortar and Pestle

pound the material in the bottom of the mortar. Once you have the material broken down into small pieces (pea-sized or smaller) you can begin to grind with the pestle by pushing down gently and stirring the material. Pressing down on the pestle and pressing it tightly against the side of the mortar will gradually powder the material.

This is a time-tested method for powdering ingredients. It is also very time-consuming. On the positive side, your arms will eventually get stronger because it requires a lot of muscle power to use the mortar and pestle for all of your grinding needs. In general, resins are easy to powder using a mortar and pestle. Frankincense, for example, can be ground to powder fairly quickly. Tough plant materials, like sage leaves for example, can take an immense amount of time to powder with a mortar and pestle.

Mill

A mill uses a pair of flat stones or steel plates to grind material to a very fine powder. Some are motorized and others are hand-powered. If you use a mill to powder your ingredients you can simply feed your coarsely ground material into the hopper. Crank it out the other side and a fine powder will result. Most mills allow you to adjust the coarseness of the material. The finer the grind the better for incense making, but the longer it will take. Resins can make quite a mess when run through a mill. Since it is easy to powder resins other ways, I'd avoid powdering them with a mill.

A mill can be as expensive as a $1,000 motorized machine or as simple as a $10 pepper mill. You can often find a pepper mill for far less than that at garage sales or thrift stores. The only drawback to a pepper mill is that they can often be very slow. My pepper mill takes about an hour to grind half a teaspoon of red cedar powder. A coffee mill is also a good choice, just make certain that it has grinding stones or plates. Many companies sell "mills" that actually chop rather than grind. Those are good too (see the next section), but they will never produce the fine powder of a mill. If you are serious about powdering your own incense ingredients, especially base materials, you will eventually need to get a mill.

Blender or Grinder

If you use a blender or a coffee grinder to powder materials, make sure everything is chopped or broken into small pieces. Large chunks of material, rocks, or large bits of wood can all damage your blender or grinder. With wood especially, you need to chop or break it into small pieces before placing inside the machine (sawdust is the ideal form to start powdering wood). Resins should always be broken into small pieces and checked for bark and rocks that need to be removed.

With hard materials, like wood bits, you can add a small amount to your grinder or blender and allow it to run for a while. On blenders you can start with a low setting and then as the material becomes finer you can move it up to full speed. Most grinders only have one speed.

If powdering soft materials, like resins, you'll want to pulse the machine rather than just allowing it to run constantly. Grind resins for three to four seconds and then stop. Check the material and grind again for three to four seconds if you need to. If you allow your machine to run continuously the resin may begin to heat up. If that happens you will end up with a sticky mess in the bottom of the machine that will take longer to clean than powdering in a mortar and pestle would have. I once had to spend three hours cleaning dragon's blood resin out of my blender. Keep resins cool and you'll find them easy to powder with any method you choose. Some incense makers even freeze resins before grinding to both make the resin harder (thus easier to grind) and to keep it cooler during grinding.

Sifting

Once you've ground your material to the finest powder you can reasonably make, you'll need to sift it. A lot of kitchens have a sifter with a handle that you crank, forcing a metal arm over the screen in the bottom. The arm forces the material through the screen. Do not use one of those sifters for making incense. When sifting incense, use a screen sifter. Put your powder inside and gently shake it. That will filter out any large bits, hard bits, or foreign matter. The finer the sifter, the finer the incense powder it will produce. Never try to force anything through the screen. If it won't flow through then don't put it in your incense. You don't want too fine a screen if you've been using a grinder or blender since they can't produce as fine a powder.

After shaking the material through the screen, you can return any large bits to your grinder and try to powder it further. Sift that material as well and add it to the first batch sifted. Never waste any incense ingredient.

Buying Powdered Ingredients

Although most incense makers agree that aromatics store best in their "whole" form, powdered just before use, buying ingredients that are already powdered has advantages. A beginning incense maker may not want to invest in a grinder or blender just for making incense. You can easily purchase many aromatics and bases already powdered. Binders are generally found only as powder. Most wood powder will be milled, and some incense experts feel that impacts their scent, but for bases using milled wood is great. You might want to chop wood you use as an aromatic.

Storing Ingredients

Once you've gone through all this effort to powder your materials, make sure to store them properly. You should store them in an airtight container. A thick plastic bag is acceptable, but a sealed jar is much better (using both is better yet). Even an old jam jar will work. You should also protect the powder from light and humidity. If you use a clear container, try storing the powder in a paper bag inside the container to protect it from the light. I have a collection of darkly colored glass containers and some earthenware as well. Don't store your containers in an area with high humidity (such as under a sink). Once powdered, no matter how well stored, the material will start to lose some of its oil so use it as soon as you can (although no incense-making material should ever be thrown away simply because it is old).

Magickal Considerations

In addition to all the other factors you consider, when making incense for ritual or magickal use you need to consider the magickal attributes of your ingredients as well. Although several times before I have stressed testing aromatics and using those with pleasant scents, you can also add ingredients that have very little scent. Additions like that allow you to add ingredients with desired magickal associations. Aromatics that have a little scent can be safely added to most blends. Just be certain that you avoid using ingredients at magickal cross-purposes. If you were making incense to honor the sign of Water, for example, you wouldn't want to use any dragon's blood as it is aligned with the sign of Fire.

Although I strongly believe that all incense needs to be pleasing to the nose, one of the joys of making incense is that you can do what pleases you. If you want to make incense that does not create a pleasing scent, strictly because of the magickal alignments of the materials, you are free to do so. Personally, I find that the unpleasant smell distracts me from the work at hand, but some incense makers tell me they experience the opposite effect and it enhances their magick. If you're a prankster, you'll even find that your incense-making skills can be used to create some pretty terrible smells (although I haven't included any recipes of that nature in this book).

Collecting Incense Materials

Collecting materials can start right in your own yard. If you trim trees in your yard, the wood might make a great base. The wood might even be an aromatic—test it with charcoal. If you trim any fruit trees you should definitely try to use the wood for your incense. The simple way is to run the branches through a chipper. You can then dry the chips and powder them as described earlier. Wild honeysuckle, dandelion root, and clover are all incense materials that you might find in your yard.

If you leave your yard and begin to collect in the wild you have to use tremendous care. There are wonderful aromatic plants that grow in the wild, but every day they become more rare. Although wild collecting is a wonderful spiritual, as well as physical, adventure you need to be very mindful of the needs of the plants. No matter how wonderful or powerful a wild plant is, collecting it could damage the chances of the species in the wild. Sometimes we have to put the needs of the plant above our own desires. That's certainly not universally true. Some wild plants grow abundantly and can be safely gathered. If you have any doubts about the rarity of a wild plant, check with your local agricultural extension office. Use your senses as well. If you see very few, or only one, plant in the area, please leave it where it is. You should also be aware that it is illegal to collect materials from most state and national parks.

You also need to keep the needs of Mother Earth in mind if you collect in the wild. If you find a plentiful aromatic growing wild in your area, use your gardening skills. Don't take a bunch of plants from one area and none from another. Collect only a few here and there to thin out the plants. That can encourage the ones you leave behind to grow further. When selecting which plants to take and which to leave, consider the impact on the surrounding plants. Are you taking a plant that offers important shade to other plants? Try to collect from the centers of plant groups and leave the fringe areas as they were.

It's even possible to use wild gathering to help Mother Earth in some rare cases. Across the world, there is a problem with invasive non-native plants in the wild. These plants often begin as imported garden plants that "escape" into the wild. Many parts of America have this problem. You might even find that your state's agricultural department has a program to eradicate such problem plants. In Oklahoma, for example, there is a volunteer program where members go out, cut down, and remove a non-native invasive cedar tree that threatens rare groves of trees on the Oklahoma plains. Cedar also happens to be a good base material (and aromatic in the case of fragrant species of cedars). You can help Mother Earth and gather incense ingredients at the same time.

How to Choose

The first factor to consider is local availability. It is always preferable to use materials that you can find in your own area. This will not only save you money (no shipping charges) but it is also more ecologically sound to use materials grown in your part of the country. Using materials you've grown is fantastic if you can do it. I find the extra energy from the process of growing the plant adds to the power of the incense.

Next, if buying materials, you need to consider the price of the material versus the quality. You can spend as much money as you'd like to buy aromatics. A higher price doesn't necessarily bring you a higher quality ingredient, but some high-priced materials are quite amazing to use. The question is, do you want to buy materials that cost more than gold? Always buy the best ingredients you can find that are affordable to you, but focus on the incense you make that works well for you. You don't need $500-an-ounce sandalwood to make wonderful sandalwood incense. Truthfully, you can make fantastic incense and never use a rare material like sandalwood at all.

You also need to consider, as mentioned earlier, what form of material you want to buy (or collect). Buying ingredients in powdered form saves a great deal of time and effort, especially for the novice incense maker. But buying and storing ingredients in their whole form gives them a much longer "shelf life" and maximum power. I recommend buying powdered woods when possible, but any material that you are confident you can powder should be bought or stored in whole form whenever possible.

The final, and often most important, factor to consider are the magickal goals you might have for your incense. Not only do you need to be aware of the magickal associations of the materials you use, but you also have to keep in mind the ethical aspects of the material. Using materials that were unethically obtained (stolen, poached, taken in a way that greatly damaged the Earth, etc.) can add negative energies to your incense. This is a difficult factor to control, as you often don't know where your materials have come from. This is another good argument for using local materials. It is much easier to assure yourself about the karma associated with the material.

Selecting incense ingredients is an important, and fun, part of the incense-making process. Locating ingredients, buying, growing, or collecting them are all steps that give you another chance to connect with your incense on a deeper level. You can't understand any of these aspects with incense that you buy. Making incense yourself is the only way to make these deep connections.

CHAPTER FIVE

TOOLS AND WORKSPACES

INCENSE MAKING REQUIRES very few tools. Actually, if you have all of your ingredients ready to roll, you are the only required tool. Your hands and your brain are the primary tools in incense making.

Tools

Nevertheless, there are some tools that make the process both easier and more fun. On the other hand, your workspace is very important and requires some careful consideration.

Gloves

I consider gloves a very important tool. You can use any kind of latex or vinyl glove. Even plastic food-service gloves will work, although they tend to slide off your hands easily. I don't like using this kind of disposable material under any circumstance, but I feel it's important for incense making. The best solution is to buy a pair of sturdy dishwashing gloves. They can be washed and reused again and again. Once you're done rolling incense you can wash the gloves just by washing your hands.

The only factor you need to consider when choosing a glove is texturing. Some gloves, especially dishwashing gloves, have raised ridges on the finger tips or the palms of the gloves. Those gloves are fine if you're molding or extruding incense, but if you're rolling the incense, the ridges will leave impressions in the incense. It shouldn't have any impact on the burning properties but it might affect the smoothness of the surface of your incense.

Some incense makers enjoy working incense with their bare hands. You can certainly do that, but take care to wash your hands well when you're finished. If you're using any oils or other materials that you are sensitive to, always wear gloves.

46

Measuring Spoons

Although incense recipes are presented in a lot of different formats, many modern incense books use teaspoons and tablespoons for measurement. This book uses that method in addition to offering recipes by weight and by ratio. Any measuring spoons will do, but metal spoons are the best choice. Plastic measuring spoons tend to hold static electricity that can make measuring and pouring more difficult.

Scales

A more precise method is to use scales and measure your incense ingredients that way. In order to make incense in the small batches the home incense maker creates, you need fairly sensitive scales. Inexpensive postal scales just won't work. A sensitive kitchen scale is a good choice. Digital scales are much easier to use but can be expensive. Get a scale that can measure half grams. Good old-fashioned triple-beam scales will also work great.

Mixing Sticks

You can use about any kind of stirrer or spoon for mixing, but I prefer wood. Wooden "craft sticks" are available at most hobby or craft stores. They are very inexpensive and work very well. If you plan to use a wooden spoon or other stirring tool repeatedly, make certain to wash it well before any incense dries on it. It can still be cleaned after the incense dries, but it is much more difficult.

Drying Board

While not mandatory, I like to use drying boards that aren't used for anything else. My own drying boards are fairly long and narrow with a raised lip on one of the long edges. That allows me to make very long sticks. But you can use many different surfaces or shapes for your drying board. Bare wood works the best, although laminated surfaces will also work. Just make sure your board is small enough to easily move and sturdy enough that it won't flex when you pick it up. In a pinch, you can even dry incense on cardboard. You might end up with a bit of paper stuck to your incense, but that's easily removed. Above all else, make sure that your drying board is clean and dry before each use.

Clay Tools

There is a dizzying array of tools on the market for working with clay and most of them are perfect for incense makers as well. You certainly don't need to buy any of these for incense making, but you might find them useful. Tools for working clay are usually quite sturdy and won't break when working with stiff incense dough. This category does not include tools designed for plastic clays (like nonhardening children's clay or "bake in your home oven" clays, both of which are much softer than natural clay). Tools for plastic clays might work, especially if they are made of metal, but there's also an excellent chance they will break under the strain of incense making. Clay tools offer a wide assortment of drilling, cutting, trimming, and scraping tools that can all be put to use in making elaborate incense shapes.

Ritual Tools

In addition to tools used to mix and shape your incense, magickal tools are quite useful, especially when making incense for ritual use. Pentacles, athames, and crystals can all be used to empower your incense. You can store the liquid you use for incense making in a chalice or a cauldron and empower it as well.

Keep in mind that your ritual tools are an important part of your craft. They should be handled with care and respect at all times. Make sure to clean them carefully once you are done using them for incense making. Dust from powders and even wet incense can get on your altar tools and should be removed at once.

Notes on Cleaning

Although you can remove dried incense from your tools, it is much simpler to clean your tools before incense dries on them. As soon as you finish rolling incense, take a few minutes to clean everything. If you reuse mixing spoons or bowls, those should be cleaned right away. Any clay tools, incense molds, and hobby knives also need to be cleaned carefully. Most importantly, if you use an extruder be certain that you clean it as soon as you finish with it. Disassemble it completely and wash each part. It only takes a few minutes and can save you a lot of headaches later. If you just don't have the time to clean your tools immediately, at least disassemble your extruder and submerge it in water. If you let the incense dry inside the extruder while it is assembled, the incense tends to glue the whole thing shut. If this happens, soak the extruder in warm water for thirty minutes and it should come apart.

Preparing Your Workspace

You don't need a large workspace and it doesn't need to be devoted to incense making all the time. It does need to be a place you can isolate if you have children or curious pets. Kitchens are often convenient to use, but any clean space (hard to find in my house!) will do.

Children and Pets

The first step in preparing your work space is planning for children and pets. Many incense-making ingredients smell interesting to children and pets, but incense is not meant for eating. It often contains things, such as wood powder, that aren't healthy to eat. Not to mention that you don't want anyone to touch the incense while it dries. For example, if you have cats and you plan to use catnip or Palo Santo in some incense, be certain to dry it where the cats can not reach. Even if they come to no harm from the incense, all of your work can be destroyed in moments. Keep drying incense and incense ingredients out of the reach of little hands, paws, and beaks.

Ventilation

I'd avoid making incense in an area without ventilation. You certainly want to keep the air flow to a minimum, but some of your powdered material will end up in the air, so it's a good idea to have a limited amount of air flow. If ventilation is a problem, consider a small air filter/cleaner. They are inexpensive and will greatly reduce the amount of powder in the air, but you should only do that if needed.

You definitely need to avoid areas with a high flow of air. Avoid air vents, intakes, or fans. All of those can help keep the air clear, but they will cause your incense to dry before you're done working with it. You really only need to worry about keeping the air clear if you're handling large quantities of powdered materials. For most home incense makers it isn't a problem.

Magickal Considerations

You have to give a little extra thought to your work area if you are making incense for magickal use. Clearing negative energies, imbuing the area with positive ones, and creating a safe place are all important factors. Don't forget that whatever energies are present as you blend and form your incense can have an impact on your final product.

Cleansing is needed in two senses of the word. You need to clean the area physically as you prepare it. You also need to clean it in a magick sense. Any negative energy present in your workspace could become part of your incense. Incense can be used to cleanse the area. Many people like to cleanse the area with sage incense, but use any scent that you feel is appropriate. If you normally use a besom around your altar, use it in your incense-making area as well. As you prepare the area, "shoo away" the negative energies that are present. These negative energies can arise from simple daily life (arguments, worries about money, etc.), so always cleanse your workspace. When making magick incense it is especially important to be able to work uninterrupted for twenty to thirty minutes. Don't forget to turn off that phone.

Once the negative energies are removed, try to add positive energies to the space. This can be accomplished by burning incense or candles that bring you happiness. You can call upon positive energies, deities, and spirits to join you in your work. To put it simply, "keep a happy thought." Dress in comfortable clothes or in ritual garb that adds to your pleasure in the experience. Once your work space is ready, take a moment and do something small that brings you joy. It can be as simple as taking a deep breath or thinking of a happy memory. It's a quick way to improve your frame of mind and thus your own energy. Finally, it's important to keep your workspace safe not only from physical hazards, but from outside influences as well. That's why it's a good idea to turn your phone's ringer off (don't forget those cell phones). Keep distracting items out of sight.

Music

A final optional, but helpful, element is music. Music lightens the heart and can have a major impact on the energy that exists within a space. It's also useful to assist you to maintain positive energies. Will your incense smell different when made with music versus no music? That's unlikely, but you might sense a different energy from incense made those two ways. It's not critical yet it can make the process even more enjoyable.

Preparing the Drying Area

Almost any area that isn't too dry (low humidity will cause your incense to dry too quickly) will work. You just need to remember a few key factors. First, make certain that you don't dry incense in sunlight (or any direct light for that matter, but sunlight does the most damage). Second, you want to avoid a place that is too warm. Although you might be tempted to pick a warm spot to make the incense dry faster, you need a place that is cool but not cold. You want a place that is reasonably free of dust with little air movement.

Extruding and Molding

If your goal is to make your own incense that smells good and burns well, you can limit yourself to rolling by hand. If you want to make truly wonderful looking incense, you might consider extruding or molding your incense. I know incense makers who roll cones by hand and have no desire to do anything else. That's great if it meets your needs. But if you want more consistency, an extruder or a mold might be in your future.

Latex Molds

Sadly, incense molds are extremely difficult to locate. Just as most incense makers guard their recipes very closely, they also tend to keep their tools a secret. Since, until recently, incense making was a well-guarded art form (and the hobby industry hasn't caught on to to this trend yet) commercial molds are almost unheard of. If you are lucky enough to find one (check the list of suppliers in Appendix B), follow the directions that come with the mold. It is much more likely that, if you want a mold, you'll need to make it yourself.

Making a Mold

If you can't find a mold, you'll need to make your own. Even someone who's never made anything like this before will find it fairly simple. One of the advantages of making your own mold is that you can make incense in the exact shape you want. It's a little extra work but it will pay off for you for many years to come as you make more and more incense with your own molds. This type of latex mold won't work well for making sticks with bamboo rods, but you'll find a neat little trick for making those at the end of this section.

1. Make a Prototype

The first step is to make a "perfect" cone. You'll want to either roll it with incense by hand or, even better, make it from clay. You need to use clay that will dry, so non-hardening children's clay won't work. There are many colorful brands of clay available that can be baked in your oven for rapid drying. Make your cone and dry or bake it completely. If you wish, you can use a commercial cone that you've purchased as your prototype. The drawback is that most commercial cones are too short and too thick. There are a couple of commercial brands that are tall and thin. They will work best. You also need to check the cone for seams. Many commercial cones are made in two-part molds that leave a seam line. You should trim or sand those off before proceeding to the next step.

Once your cone is ready, you need a bit of scrap wood or heavy cardboard. A piece of wood about two inches square is perfect. Using ordinary white glue, attach the bottom of the cone to the center of the board. If you're using actual incense as your prototype, also apply a thin coat of glue over the surface of the cone in order to seal it. If you used clay for your prototype this step shouldn't be needed. Allow the cone and wood to dry completely (at least twenty-four hours, maybe more).

2. Use Liquid Latex

There are several brands of liquid latex on the market today. You can find it at your local hobby supplier or on the web. If you're only planning to use it for this one project, buy the smallest container you can find. It will take very little latex to make a single cone mold. You'll also need a small, soft paint brush but don't buy an expensive one. A cheap one will work just fine. Always follow the directions on the latex that you buy. The following instructions will work with any latex that I've seen, but if what I say disagrees with the label on your latex, follow the label.

Brush a thin coat of latex over the entire cone and on the surface of the wood or cardboard. If you're using a piece that is two inches by two inches, brush the latex over the entire top surface right up to the edges. Don't brush any latex beyond the top of the board. Immediately wipe off any latex that might run down the sides of the board with a damp cloth. Wash your brush according to label directions.

Allow the first coat to dry completely (check the label on your latex to see how long that might take). Apply a second and a third coat in the exact same way. Once the third coat is completely dry you can proceed to the next step. It only takes a minute or two to apply a coat, although it might take an hour or more for each layer to dry.

51

3. Support with Gauze

After the third layer is dry you need to measure a little gauze. Lay out a flat strip or two onto the surface of the wood. You'll need to make a small cutout on the gauze to allow room for the cone that is mounted on the board. Also wrap a piece of gauze around the entire surface of the cone as well. You don't want to use any more gauze on the cone than is needed to cover it completely. The gauze on the bottom should be a little longer than the wood itself so that some hangs over the edge.

52 Once you've cut the gauze, apply another thin coat of latex. As soon as that coat is on, carefully press the gauze in place into the wet latex. Don't worry if there's a little extra gauze during this step. Once the gauze gets wet it might stretch more than it did when dry. That's easy to fix later on. After the gauze is pressed into the latex, apply another very thin coat over it to make certain all of the gauze is wet.

After the gauze layer dries (give it twenty-four hours to dry completely), apply two more thin coats of latex. All of that latex combined with the gauze layer will give you a strong mold that will last a long time. After the final coat of latex has completely dried, dust it lightly with some talcum powder. That will keep the latex from sticking to itself later. Don't leave any loose talc on the mold so blow or wipe off the excess powder. Firmly grasp one of the overhanging pieces of gauze. Carefully peel the mold away from the wood. Do this all the way around the mold until the base is totally free from the wood. Then gently and evenly loosen and remove the cone.

4. Slit the Side

Your mold is almost ready! Hopefully you were able to remove the mold from the cone without turning the mold inside out. But if it did flip around, you can poke it back the right way. That's why the dusting of talcum powder is so important. The final step is to take a pair of sharp scissors and cut a single slit. Begin on the center edge of one side of the base and make a single cut straight up to the tip of the cone. The slit will allow you to open the mold later and remove the wet cone.

It seems like a lot of work when you can just roll cones by hand, but the whole process can be done in three days. And you won't need more than an hour or two during those three days since most of the three days is needed for drying time.

Extruders

To make nice professional-looking sticks and coils you need an extruder. An extruder is basically a tool to "squirt out" incense dough. There are a lot of gadgets out there to do this for cake decorating and you might be tempted to use one of those for incense making. I have tried this with many, many cooking devices and I've learned that most of them are simply too weak to use with incense making. You can forget using anything with significant plastic parts in it. Plastic isn't strong enough to use with incense dough. Cake decorating bags aren't strong enough either, although you can make a very simple extruder by finding a very thick plastic bag and cutting one corner off. You can squeeze your dough out the hole, but the bags usually split after only a few minutes use. The only kitchen devices that might work are cookie presses. Cookie dough is often even harder and thicker than incense dough and cookie presses are designed with that in mind. Don't waste time on a plastic one, but some are made of metal and might be adaptable to incense making. But most cookie presses are used with large batches and we make incense in small batches. Keep in mind that once you make incense with it, your cookie press can't ever make cookies again.

53

The simplest extruders that are strong enough to work are those made for clay. Visit your local hobby shop and go to the clay area. You should find several brands of "clay guns." A clay gun is basically a metal syringe and plunger with an assortment of tips to extrude clay in different shapes. They usually range in price from $5 to $25. These will work well as incense extruders with one exception. The tips are usually flat disks with holes cut in their center. Different shaped holes give different shaped clay. Unfortunately, incense dough doesn't flow the same way the plastic clays do. Clay comes out of these extruders in smooth streams, but incense dough will often come out with a very rough and jagged surface. This can be remedied by briefly rolling the incense to smooth the surface.

Extruders: "Clay Gun"

An even better way is to modify your clay gun slightly. Incense is extruded smoothly by using a tapered tip rather than a flat one. My first extruder was a clay gun of this type. At the same time, I had purchased a plastic syringe used for giving liquid medicine to babies. The plastic syringe broke very soon under the strain, but its tapered tip never failed. I cut this one-inch tapered tip from the bottom of the plastic syringe and inserted it into the tip of my clay gun. The result was the finest, smoothest spaghetti sticks you've ever seen.

Using this type of extruder you will be able to make not only wonderful spaghetti sticks but long coils in any shape you wish. You can even use an extruder like this to write with incense. Writing someone's name in incense is always an eye-opening gift. It's a simple project to build this type of extruder and definitely worth the effort. You can make incense on par with any incense professional.

Personally, I use a much larger extruder built from a caulking gun. I don't have space in this book to explain how to build one of these extruders, but if you're handy in the shop I'm sure you can figure it out. If you're not, then I wouldn't bother trying. The clay gun style of extruder is all most incense makers will ever need.

Straw Molds

This is a simple way to make a mold for either spaghetti sticks or sticks with bamboo rods. Take a clean plastic drinking straw and split it all the way down the edge. You can then load the inside of the straw with your wet dough. Pack it in well and make sure to get all the air bubbles out of the straw. At this point you can add a bamboo rod or toothpick if you wish. Then, with the edges of the slit slightly overlapping, press the outside of the straw firmly and evenly so that the dough is tightly packed. Let the straw sit for five to twenty minutes and then peel the straw off the incense. If it has set up well enough you might be able to slide it out of the straw.

You might be tempted to dry the sticks inside the straws but don't. Without an airspace around the dough it won't dry and will eventually mildew. If you wish to dry it in a straw, remove it from your straw mold and insert the incense into a larger straw so that there is an air space. It's tough to find straws of a good size, but it is an inexpensive and easy way to mold spaghetti sticks, cylinders, or sticks with rods.

The tools and workspace for incense making are not complicated. Molds and extruders are a lot of fun, but they're purely optional. You just need to look around your house and you'll find most of the tools you'll want. A little thought needs to go into your workspace, but all homes have a few great places. Although preparing the area for making ritual incense seems, on the surface, to be a lot more complicated it really isn't. Just keep positive energies around you and you'll do fine.

CHAPTER SIX

MAKING INCENSE

ALL RIGHT, YOU'VE selected your materials, prepared your work space and gathered your tools. It's time to roll your first batch of incense. Make sure you have everything you need and unplug the telephone. About half an hour is all you'll need, but once you start it's best not to be interrupted.

Selecting a Recipe

There are two aspects to selecting a recipe. The first, and most important, factor is the materials available to you. Do a quick inventory of what herbs, resins, and wood you have in your cupboard and compare that to your recipes. Some incense blends are created simply because those were the items the incense maker had on hand.

The second thing to consider when picking a recipe is the desired result. Do you want a floral or an earthy scent? Something bright or something dark? If you know that there is a particular type of scent that you want to make, look through your recipes and find some that sound good to you. Find a recipe that you can make with what you have on hand or that you only need one or two items for. You can then seek those materials out before trying to make the incense. If the recipe sounds truly appealing or something that you just have to try then it will be worth the effort to find the missing ingredients. The journey itself is often worth the trip.

When making magickal incense, a little more consideration should be given to your recipe selection. If you are making incense for ritual or spell work, the ingredients need to complement that work. Although I caution against using any ingredient that you dislike just because of its magickal associations, take care not to use anything that might run counter to your goals either.

Mixing the Dry Ingredients

Although some other incense books put forward the idea of mixing your binder with water to form a glue and then adding aromatics to that glue, I don't care for that method. The dry mixing method is easier and much more reliable, although you can use the wet mixing method if you are familiar with it.

Blending

Combine all of your powdered aromatics, base material, and binder in a bowl. Mix with a wooden stick or spoon. This is an important step and shouldn't be rushed. Carefully stir and blend until the powder is a single, consistent color. If you notice any lumps in the mixture, take care to break those up and mix them into the powder. Lumps like that can impair your incense's ability to burn. Lumps often form in powdered material, especially resins, when they are stored. If you notice a lot of lumps while you are mixing, sift your mixture before proceeding.

Some incense makers go so far as to mix their powdered ingredients in a mortar and then crush and mix them at the same time. This is an extra step that isn't required but may well improve the quality of your incense. This is a part of the process that you can control when you make your own incense and is one of the great things about doing it yourself.

Another way to improve the quality of your incense is to carefully blend your powdered ingredients but leave the binder out. Once blended, put the mixture into a sealed container, preferably one that is dark colored or blocks out light altogether. Then allow the mixture to sit in a cool (but not cold) dry place for one to three months. You can let it sit for even longer than that if desired. This allows the various scents to blend. This is another extra step that can really improve your incense. Just don't forget to add your binder before adding the liquid. It's best not to add in the binder from the start because gum binders can cause clumping, although if you use makko it should be aged along with the rest of the mixture.

Visualization

During the mixing process you have an excellent opportunity to "orient" the energies of your incense. You can do this through basic visualization. As you mix the incense, imagine the desired result from your incense. If you are making incense for a prosperity spell, visualize (see with your mind's eye) the financial outcome you need. If making incense for love, imagine the perfect relationship with the person you love. Even when making incense for mundane use, imagine the happy life you cherish or the love you have for the person that will receive the incense.

This process of visualization gives shape to the energy in the incense. Without visualization, the energy in your incense will still be released, it just won't be focused. That's fine if you merely want to energize a space, but to achieve specific goals with your incense, visualize your goals throughout the incense making process. It's a great way to share your love.

Empowerment

Incense itself contains power. The power in the plants that you have used also exists in your incense. The many days of sunshine and rain, the seasons of many years, and many full moons passed are all stored in your incense ingredients. This is one of the reasons that it is so important to use natural ingredients in your incense and to handle them with respect and love. These plants and trees have, in some cases, given their lives for you to make this incense. Cherish that energy. Respect it and the plants that have helped you. Never be careless or wasteful of that energy.

In addition to using visualization to orient the energy inherent in your incense, you can also add to that energy. This process occurs naturally to a limited extent as you mix the incense anyway. Blending and kneading transfers energy from you to your incense. You can also add even more energy by channeling energy from yourself into the incense as you mix. Energy can also be transferred from ritual tools, especially athames. Place your mixing bowl over the tool and, using visualization, see the energy in your tool moving into the incense. You wouldn't want to do this routinely (or your tools will never get the chance to build up more energy), but it is a useful method for maximizing your incense's power.

Other important factors in the empowerment of your incense are when and where it is made. Mixing incense under a full moon or within a magick circle will obviously add to the power of your incense. I've also found that incense is far more energized when mixed and even rolled in places of power. The next time you venture into the woods, take some incense making ingredients with you and blend the powder in some special little spot. If possible, add something from the place where you mix it, be that a bit of leaf or bark or even some water collected and used later to roll the incense. We all have places where our energy is maximized. Mix your incense there and it will receive some of that energy as well. Is it mandatory to make incense under such special conditions? Certainly not, you can make incense any time of the day or year. It is simply a way to provide maximum energy to your efforts.

58

If properly charged, your incense can act as a magickal battery. There are many ways to maximize that energy, but maximizing it isn't nearly as important as focusing it. A great deal of energy with no purpose can do as much harm as good, so be certain to use your visualization skills when making any incense blend, even for mundane use.

Adding Liquid

Whether you're using a "traditional" recipe, a recipe from this book, or even one you've created yourself, it's important to always begin with less water (or other liquids) than is called for in the recipe. Such subtle factors as the temperature of the room, humidity, or water temperature can have an impact on the amount of water needed. It is easy to add more water if the mix is too dry but it's difficult to remove water if you put in too much.

Once you're ready to add the water (either immediately after mixing all the dry ingredients or after aging the blend and lastly adding in your binder), begin by adding about three-quarters of the total amount of water called for in the recipe. Carefully blend and mix the water in. It could take up to five minutes. At first it may look like you have a lot of dry powder and not enough water, but keep mixing. As you mix, press the mixture together to help force the water into dry areas. You'll be surprised how little water some recipes require.

As you stir, the mix will begin to look a lot like unrolled pie dough. It will often break into small balls of material. Some ingredients might not act that way, but most will. Once it reaches this stage, or if you've mixed the blend for several minutes, put on your gloves and use your hands to gather the incense "dough" into a single lump. If the ball won't stick together, add a little more water. Even if the mix is too dry you should be able to gather it into your hand. Once you can do that, begin kneading the mixture with your hands. After kneading for several minutes, try rolling the dough into a single large ball in your hands. If you can form a ball, look at the surface of it. Is it smooth and free of cracks? If so, then you're ready to form your incense. If not, add another ⅛ teaspoon of water and knead again for at least thirty seconds. You never want to use too much water, so only exceed the amount of water in the recipe if you are absolutely certain you need it.

Patience is very important at this stage. Always make sure you knead the dough thoroughly after each addition of water. It is surprising what a difference a tiny bit of water will make in your mixture. Kneading disperses the water throughout your mixture. Adding too much water makes your incense hard to handle and shape. If you do accidentally add too much water, check chapter 9 ("Troubleshooting") for tips on salvaging your dough.

59

Adding Oils

If you plan to add oils to your incense this would be the proper time to do that. Roll the dough into a single ball and check for cracks. If it looks acceptable, make an impression in the dough with your thumb. Add a few drops of oil into the impression and carefully fold the dough over the top. Then knead for several minutes to disperse the oil evenly throughout the dough.

Handling Wet Incense

Once you have your dough ready to roll, there are a few basic things you need to keep in mind while your incense is in the wet form. Once your incense dries it will reflect how it was handled when it was wet. You'll be greatly rewarded from having a well prepared work and drying area for your incense.

Any time you are handling wet incense you should wear gloves. This is particularly important if you've added any oils to the mixture. Wet incense is sticky and will cling to your skin. Any oils you've added or even natural oils in the materials you've used can enter your body through the skin. But mostly it is a big mess. I must admit that on occasion I do mix incense with bare skin for a more intimate connection with the incense, but I wouldn't make a regular habit of it.

It's important to work with your incense dough in a generally clean area. It's really a good idea to work over a floor that can be mopped. Clean the floor around the area where you'll handle the dough. This is to protect your incense in the event that you drop it. Dropping wet incense on a floor that is less than completely clean will result in incense with lint or hair in the mix. It's virtually impossible to clean these things off your wet incense and burning hair is never a good aromatic.

Another important tip on cleanliness is to always clean your drying and work surfaces between batches. If you've dried incense on a board, there are often small bits and powder leftover on the board. If you lay wet incense on that material it will bond to the surface of the incense. That's not a problem if you are still making the same scent, but if you're using a different blend you don't want the "leftovers" from the last batch clinging to the new one.

60

Once you've activated the binder in your mix by adding water (or other liquids) you have a limited amount of time to make your incense. Since you've added the least amount of water possible, your incense will start to dry at once. If you don't shape it yourself, it will dry in whatever shape you leave it in. That's why it's a good idea to unplug the phone and close the door and give yourself thirty minutes to make your incense. But life doesn't always cooperate with our plans. If you have to leave your wet incense for more than just a few minutes, cover it with a damp paper towel. If you're going to be away for more than just a few minutes, you should also consider putting your covered dough into a sealed container (like a glass jar). Even sealed like that, you shouldn't let it sit for more than a few hours. Oftentimes, mold begins to grow on the wet incense in as little as an hour. Even if you can't see it, the mold on the surface of your incense will get mixed into your blend when you return to rolling or extruding it. Worse yet, some blends will visibly mold in as little time as overnight. It's a sad loss to something that required a lot of care and effort.

It's also important to remember to visualize throughout the process. If you have a problem or drop something, don't allow yourself to become upset. Any negative energy you channel into your incense will be released when burned, just like positive energy. Listen to music that makes you happy, keep a positive thought and enjoy the incense-making process. The end result will be incense with power impossible to find in any "off-the-shelf" incense.

Rolling Incense

The shaping of incense "dough" is one of the most fun aspects of incense making. Choose the form (or forms) that interest you and start forming the dough into its final shapes. Although incense will shrink a bit as it dries, the shape you create is the form your finished incense will retain.

Cones

The most basic, and undoubtedly most ancient, technique for shaping incense is using your hands. You can roll a simple cone with this easy method. First, pinch off a bit of incense dough (¼ teaspoon or less). You can use the thumb and index finger of both your hands around the dough to form it into a tall, thin, four-sided pyramid. If it is thin enough, this shape will work for many recipes.

You can refine this simple shape very easily by taking the pyramid and rolling it using the palm of one hand as a rolling surface and the index finger of the other hand to roll it back and forth. Put your finger parallel over the cone so that your finger totally covers up the cone. Then roll the cone back and forth quickly and it will round off the edges, making the cone shape we all know. It will also make the cone taller and thinner (which will improve its burning properties). Pinch off the top ¼ of the cone (which is usually very thin) and leave the top flat. You can then press the thick end of the cone down on your drying board (as if you were setting it down to burn it). Pressing it down will often cause the bottom to flair out a little. That probably won't have much of an effect on the way the incense burns, but if you don't like the way that looks you can use a razor blade or hobby knife to cut a nice flat bottom for your cone. Your cone should have a base no thicker than an unsharpened pencil and be 1½ to 2½ inches tall.

Spaghetti Sticks/Cylinders

There are several ways to make spaghetti sticks and cylinders by hand. The most obvious is to break off some of your dough and roll it between your hands or on a flat surface—just like playing with clay when you were a kid! The hardest part of rolling spaghetti sticks and cylinders this way is getting them to a consistent thickness. These types of cylinders will frequently vary in thickness along their entire length. As long as the cylinders aren't too thick they will still burn just fine. With practice you'll be able to roll very even cylinders.

Another technique that works well is more of a baker's approach to incense making. I've known incense makers who use this method with great effectiveness. Take your dough and roll it out flat. You can use a rolling pin (just remember that you won't be able to use it for food making ever again), a bit of dowel rod or even pipe. Once rolled out (you might want to do that on wax paper or foil) you can then cut strips. A rolling pizza cutter works well for this purpose, but a simple plastic knife or even a toothpick will work just fine. You can leave your incense in strip form or you can take the strips and roll them lightly by hand to round off the edges. It's best to cut the strips at a width equal to the thickness of your dough. That will give you a nice square stick that's easy to round off and it will dry evenly.

Sticks

By this I mean sticks with bamboo rods up the center. I don't recommend this form, but a lot of novice incense makers want to make this type of incense. The easiest way to make this style incense is by making a spaghetti stick or even a cylinder as described earlier and then inserting the bamboo rod through the center. Once you've done that it's a really good idea to go back and press the dough (or better, lightly roll it) onto the stick to make certain that it adheres to the wood. An important key to creating a stick of this type that will actually burn well is to use a very thin bamboo rod. The simplest way to do that is to buy some bamboo skewers at your grocery store and then slice one apart with a razor blade or hobby knife. As always, use great care when handling a sharp blade. Use the thinnest rod you can that is strong enough to support the incense.

An alternative to putting a rod all the way through the center is the toothpick method. Make a cylinder a bit thicker than an average incense stick. Then insert an ordinary round-tipped toothpick into one end of the cylinder. Press it in about halfway. This way, you get the advantages of having the wooden rod without the disadvantage of trying to make it burn. You stand a much better chance of creating a stick that will burn well.

Using a Latex Cone Mold

If you've gone through all the trouble to make a mold, you'll want to use it correctly. Your mold will be unique, so you might find your own tricks to using it but these instructions will give a great idea of how to make it work best for you.

1. Taping

This first step is optional but a really good idea for the first few times you use it. Use a piece of cellophane tape and wrap it around the thickest part of the cone section to hold the slit closed. Once you've made some cones with the mold you might want to skip this step as it slows the process down quite a bit.

2. Watering

Add a drop or two of water to the inside of your taped mold. Use the tip of your finger or a cotton swab to evenly spread a thin layer of water around the whole inside of the mold. This will help the incense come out of the mold a lot easier. If your incense mix is particularly wet you can skip this step.

3. Packing

The next step is to pack the mold. Hold the mold with your thumb over the slit in the side. Even when taped, the mold can open slightly as you pack it and having your thumb in place helps hold the seam closed. Press your wet incense dough into the mold. It's best to make the rough four-sided pyramid shape discussed in the rolling section and then insert that into the mold. That will create the fewest air spaces. Press dough into the mold until it is full but not overfull. An overfilled mold will distort the shape. Any excess dough sticking out beyond the base of the mold can be scraped or cut off to form a flat bottom.

4. Releasing

The final step is to remove (or release) the incense from the mold. Remove the tape from the mold, if used, and open the mold at the slit. Open the mold as far as you can. You can then turn the mold upside down with your free hand beneath it and shake the cone out of the mold. You may get better results by opening the mold and carefully removing the incense by its base. Once removed from the mold, you can then place the cone on your drying board.

Using an Extruder

You may find that you need to reformulate your recipes slightly. Extra water might be needed and using warm water can help. If you use warm water you'll want to extrude the incense quickly, before it cools too much. Once it cools it gets much stiffer and harder to extrude.

Assemble your extruder according to the directions (adding a tapered tip if possible). Roll your dough into a cylinder thin enough to fit into the extruder and fill the extruder halfway. If you find you have trouble applying enough pressure to extrude the incense reduce the amount of dough that you use. A clay gun only $1/4$ full should be easy enough to extrude that anyone can do it. Insert the plunger and extrude your sticks directly onto your drying board. You can cut your sticks to length while wet or wait until they dry. You can also extrude incense in coils. This is a great way to make a long stick since it takes up much less space. Coils are also less effected by the problems of curling.

Always clean your extruder when you finish using it. Incense dough washes off easily. Clean all the parts and dry it disassembled. If you allow it to dry with the dough inside of

63

it, you might end up with some mildew problems or worse yet, your gun might be "glued" shut. If this happens, just let the extruder soak in hot water for half an hour and you should be able to easily take it apart and clean it properly.

Drying Incense

This is the most important and difficult aspect of the incense-making process. Incense dried too quickly may severely distort, crack or just fail to burn. Incense dried too slowly can mildew. Drying your incense is critical to its success and it is a balance of three key ingredients: temperature, humidity, and time.

Temperature

You will be tempted to put your wet incense in a hot room, direct sunlight, or even an oven in order to dry it. This is a major mistake often made by new incense makers. The drying step is one that can't be rushed. One of the popular incense books on the market actually recommends drying your incense in a closed car. It may dry faster but the result will be inferior and might even fail to burn.

One of the common effects of drying incense too quickly is cracking. When a cone cracks it often fails to burn. You can light it and it will send out smoke through the crack. Once the burning surface reaches the wide point on the crack, the cone will usually go out. There can be other causes for cracking (primarily using too little binder, see chapter 9), but fast drying is one of them. Cracked incense won't burn properly.

Drying too fast can also cause severe distortions in your incense. All incense shrinks as it dries and this can lead to distortions in the shape, but fast drying can exaggerate the problem. Slow drying will help to minimize distortions.

If you have put oils into your incense, drying at a high temperature or low humidity can cause the oils to evaporate from your incense. That's not only wasteful but will keep you from achieving the desired effect with the oil. If you've used a special liquid in place of water in your recipes, its benefits can also be evaporated right out of the incense in a hot environment.

It's unlikely that your drying area would be too cool. Around fifty degrees Fahrenheit is an excellent temperature. Cooler than that will still work, but you obviously can't dry incense below the freezing point. Never dry your incense in direct sunlight. That will change the chemical properties in your incense and might radically affect the scent.

Humidity

Again, you might be tempted to dry your incense in an area with as little humidity as possible. Too low a humidity may cause your incense to dry too quickly just like a high temperature. Loss of oils, cracking, and all the other problems mentioned earlier can occur with low humidity as well.

Although humidity is only a serious problem in extremes (very low or very high), 50–60 percent works great. Don't worry too much if your humidity is not in that range, but avoid the extreme ends of the scale.

Time

This is the single most important aspect of the drying process. I know your urge will be to dry your incense as quickly as possible so that you can try out the fruits of your labor. Don't give in to that temptation. Let your incense dry slowly and be patient. Give your spaghetti sticks a minimum of two days to dry (dry them even slower than that if you can). Allow cones a minimum of three days to dry with a week being ideal. You'll have to closely monitor the temperature and humidity if you want to dry incense that slowly.

Your patience will be rewarded. If you try to burn your incense before it dries completely it will go out soon after you light it. Once you've lit it, you might never be able to dry it properly and all of that work will have been wasted. If you try to burn one stick and it goes out, it might not be finished drying. Give the rest of the batch another twenty-four hours to dry before testing again.

Preparing your drying area can be a little tricky, but don't sweat the details too much. Most incense will dry just fine on your kitchen counter (keep it away from sinks and heat sources). A clean kitchen cabinet is often just right. Humidity and temperature are relatively easy to control and patience is a skill that incense making will teach you if you haven't learned it already.

Your First Batch of Incense

You've studied hard and now it's time for that effort to pay off. Is your incense-making area prepared? Have you gathered your ingredients and tools and unplugged the phone? All right, let's put on the gloves and roll some incense!

Here's the simplest incense recipe you could ask for and it yields wonderful results. Mix together 7½ teaspoons of powdered sandalwood (or other fragrant wood powder) with ¼ teaspoon of guar gum or gum tragacanth or 1 teaspoon of makko. The total amount of water called for in this recipe is 4¼ teaspoons, so add only ¾ of that amount to your dry mix and add the remainder of the water ⅛ teaspoon at a time until your dough is the right consistency.

Once you can roll the dough into a ball with no significant cracks in it, you can roll the incense out. You don't need a mold or an extruder, you can just roll your sticks and cones with your hands. That's the most fun anyway. Once you've tried this very simple but wonderful recipe I bet you'll be eager to find some more elaborate recipes. In no time you'll have the most wonderful smelling house on the block and tons of handmade gifts for your friends and family.

CHAPTER SEVEN

RECIPES

ALL BUT THE first section of recipes in this book have been divided based on the binder used. The first section is simple incense using only a single aromatic. The second section is complex recipes that use gum binders (guar gum or gum tragacanth). The third section is complex recipes that use makko as the binder. The final section contains recipes for moist incense.

How to Use the Recipes

The recipes are in an easy-to-use format. Each recipe is given in three different ways. The first way is by volume. To use that column, you will need a set of measuring spoons. By looking down that column you will see how many teaspoons or tablespoons you need of each ingredient. Personally, this is my preferred method. The second way is by weight. To use that column you will need a set of scales that can measure half grams. Just weigh out the appropriate amount of each ingredient.

The final method is by ratio. Many incense makers prefer to write their recipes in terms of a ratio. The ratio version of the recipe is given in "parts." To use that version of the recipe you can select any measurement you choose as your "part." The recipe for allspice incense is shown with this ratio: red sandalwood 2 parts, gum powder 1 part, water 15 parts, and allspice powder 20 parts. If you have a teaspoon, for example, you could use the teaspoon as your "part." So using your teaspoon, the recipe would be 2 teaspoons red sandalwood, 1 teaspoon gum powder, 15 teaspoons water, and 20 teaspoons allspice (that's for illustration purposes only—it would make a huge amount of incense!). If, instead, you wanted to use a thimble as your "part," the recipe would be 2 thimbles of red sandalwood, 1 thimble of gum powder, 15 thimbles of water, and 20 thimbles of allspice. This is especially useful for people who live in a country that doesn't use either of the other two measuring systems. It is also useful for making very small or very large batches. You could use a very tiny measure as your "part" ($^1/_{10}$ of a gram for example) or something very large (such as a gallon).

68

Whichever of the three methods you choose, you should get equally good results. If you use the ratio recipe to make a large batch of incense, you might reduce the ratio of binder slightly. You never want to use more binder than is absolutely needed. You might notice that the different versions of the recipes (volume, weight, and ratio) may not all give you the exact same result. The recipe for "Four Quarters," for example, might come out with slightly different results when made using the volume recipe as compared to the weight recipe. The results will be wonderful no matter which method you choose.

A Note on Using Measuring Spoons

If you use measuring spoons, it's important to understand how to use them correctly. Select the appropriately sized spoon and use it to scoop the powdered ingredient. The spoon should be full, with powder piled above the top of the spoon. You then need to use something with a level edge (a mixing stick, notecard, ruler, business card, etc.) to scrape the excess material from the spoon. Place the straight-edge on the top of the spoon and drag it across the top, scraping the excess material down to the same level as the top of the spoon. This ensures that you measure the exact same amount every time. If you don't fill the spoon completely, you won't have enough material. If you fill the spoon above its top, then you will have too much material. By scraping the powder down to the level of the top of the spoon you will get the same amount every time (this is called a "level spoonful").

Finally, understand that these recipes are only a guide. Feel free to modify the recipes to fit your needs or the ingredients you have available. Just be aware that changing the ingredients might result in recipes that won't work. See chapter 8 for details on modifying recipes and experimenting. You may also find that you need to adjust the amounts in the recipes slightly to better suit your own ingredients. The amount of moisture in your powdered ingredients can affect both the weight and volume of the powder, so be sure to keep your ingredients as dry as possible.

If you wish, you can substitute gum arabic for guar gum or tragacanth, but you should at least triple the amount called for in the recipe. Gum arabic is weak, although it is quite sticky. You can also use a different wood powder as your base. I have included red cedar and pine as bases in some of the recipes and those will work fine. But for the best results you might consider replacing pine with sandalwood and red cedar with red sandalwood. Pine and red cedar are acceptable for beginning incense makers, but sandalwood is usually the superior choice.

All of these recipes have been tested both as spaghetti sticks and as cones and should work fine in either form. Having said that, spaghetti sticks always burn better and I hope you will make those far more often than cones. Variations in ingredients might make your incense a bit harder to burn. If your cones won't burn, try them upside down or roll spaghetti sticks instead. With many of the recipes, you can reduce (or even eliminate) the clove in the recipe if you make spaghetti sticks rather than cones.

Simple Recipes

Recipes with only one aromatic are very useful. Not only are they easier to make, they are great substitutes for herbs burned alone on charcoal. Simple recipes are also a perfect choice if you plan to do any "air mixing" (see Appendix D for details).

Allspice		VOLUME	WEIGHT	RATIO
Base	Red sandalwood	½ tsp	.5g	2
Binder	Guar gum or tragacanth	¼ tsp	1g	1
Liquid	Water	3¾ tsp	17.5g	15
Aromatic	Allspice	5 tsp	10g	20

Bay		VOLUME	WEIGHT	RATIO
Base	Sandalwood	1 Tbsp	6g	12
Binder	Guar gum or tragacanth	¼ tsp	1g	1
Liquid	Water	4½ tsp	19.5g	22
Aromatic	Bay	1¼ tsp	2.5g	5

Cinnamon (Cassia)

		VOLUME	WEIGHT	RATIO
Base	Red sandalwood	2 tsp	2.5g	8
Binder	Guar gum or tragacanth	¼ tsp	1g	1
Liquid	Water	4¼ tsp	18g	17
Aromatic	Cinnamon	4 tsp	10g	16

70

Copal

		VOLUME	WEIGHT	RATIO
Base	Red sandalwood	10 tsp	14.5g	20
Binder	Guar gum or tragacanth	½ tsp	2g	1
Liquid	Water	10 tsp	44g	20
Aromatic	Copal	2½ tsp	6g	5

Damiana

		VOLUME	WEIGHT	RATIO
Base	Sandalwood	½ tsp	1g	2
Binder	Guar gum or tragacanth	¼ tsp	1g	1
Liquid	Water or herbal tea	3¼ tsp	15g	13
Aromatic	Damiana	5 tsp	7.5g	20

Dragon's Blood

		VOLUME	WEIGHT	RATIO
Base	Red cedar	2 tsp	1.5g	16
	Clove	½ tsp	.5g	4
Binder	Guar gum or tragacanth	⅛ tsp	.5g	1
Liquid	Water	2¼ tsp	11g	18
Aromatic	Dragon's blood	½ tsp	1g	4

Frankincense

		VOLUME	WEIGHT	RATIO
Base	Sandalwood	2 Tbsp	11.5g	24
Binder	Guar gum or tragacanth	1/4 tsp	1g	1
Liquid	Water	1 Tbsp	13g	12
Aromatic	Frankincense	1 tsp	2g	4

Galangal

		VOLUME	WEIGHT	RATIO
Base	Sandalwood	2 tsp	4g	16
Binder	Guar gum or tragacanth	1/8 tsp	.5g	1
Liquid	Water	2 tsp	9.5g	16
Aromatic	Galangal	3/4 tsp	1.5g	6

Goldenseal

		VOLUME	WEIGHT	RATIO
Base	Sandalwood	2 1/4 tsp	4.5g	17
Binder	Guar gum or tragacanth	1/8 tsp	.5g	1
Liquid	Water	2 1/4 tsp	11g	17
Aromatic	Goldenseal	1 tsp	2.5g	8

Hops

		VOLUME	WEIGHT	RATIO
Base	Red sandalwood	1 Tbsp	4g	24
	Clove	1 tsp	2.5g	8
Binder	Guar gum or tragacanth	1/8 tsp	.5g	1
Liquid	Water	2 1/4 tsp	11g	17
Aromatic	Hops	1/2 tsp	.5g	4

Lavender

		VOLUME	WEIGHT	RATIO
Base	Red cedar	1 Tbsp	2.5g	12
Binder	Guar gum or tragacanth	1/4 tsp	1g	1
Liquid	Water or herbal tea	4 1/2 tsp	19.5g	18
Aromatic	Lavender	5 1/2 tsp	7.5g	22

Lemon Grass

		VOLUME	WEIGHT	RATIO
Base	Makko	2 tsp	3g	8
	Clove	1/4 tsp	.5g	1
Liquid	Water	2 1/4 tsp	11g	9
Aromatic	Lemon grass	3/4 tsp	.5g	3

Marjoram

		VOLUME	WEIGHT	RATIO
Base	Pine	2 tsp	1.5g	16
Binder	Guar gum or tragacanth	1/8 tsp	.5g	1
Liquid	Water	2 tsp	9.5g	16
Aromatic	Marjoram	1 tsp	1.5g	8

Mugwort

		VOLUME	WEIGHT	RATIO
Base	Sandalwood	2 tsp	4g	16
Binder	Guar gum or tragacanth	1/8 tsp	.5g	1
Liquid	Water	1 Tbsp	13.5g	24
Aromatic	Mugwort	1 tsp	1g	8

Myrrh

		VOLUME	WEIGHT	RATIO
Base	Red sandalwood	5 tsp	7g	20
Binder	Guar gum or tragacanth	1/4 tsp	1g	1
Liquid	Water	1 Tbsp	13.5g	12
Aromatic	Myrrh	2 tsp	4g	8

Patchouli

		VOLUME	WEIGHT	RATIO
Base	Sandalwood	1/2 tsp	1g	2
Binder	Guar gum or tragacanth	1/4 tsp	1g	1
Liquid	Water or herbal tea	3 1/2 tsp	16g	14
Aromatic	Patchouli	5 tsp	7.5g	20

Rosemary

		VOLUME	WEIGHT	RATIO
Base	Pine	2 1/2 tsp	1.5g	20
Binder	Guar gum or tragacanth	1/8 tsp	.5g	1
Liquid	Water	1 Tbsp	13.5g	24
Aromatic	Rosemary	1/2 tsp	<.5g	4

Saffron

		VOLUME	WEIGHT	RATIO
Base	Sandalwood	2 tsp	4g	16
Binder	Makko	1 tsp	1.5g	8
Liquid	Water	2 tsp	9.5g	16
Aromatic	Saffron	1/8 tsp	<.5g	1

Sage

		VOLUME	WEIGHT	RATIO
Base	Sandalwood	2 1/2 tsp	5g	10
Binder	Guar gum or tragacanth	1/4 tsp	1g	1
Liquid	Water or herbal tea	5 tsp	20.5g	20
Aromatic	Sage	7 tsp	7.5g	28

Spikenard

		VOLUME	WEIGHT	RATIO
Base	Sandalwood	1 Tbsp	6g	24
Binder	Guar gum or tragacanth	1/8 tsp	.5g	1
Liquid	Water	1 Tbsp	13.5g	24
Aromatic	Spikenard	3/4 tsp	.5g	6

Star Anise

		VOLUME	WEIGHT	RATIO
Base	Makko	1 Tbsp	4.5g	12
Liquid	Water	2 3/4 tsp	13g	19
Aromatic	Star anise	3/4 tsp	1g	3

Valerian

		VOLUME	WEIGHT	RATIO
Base	Sandalwood	1 Tbsp	6g	12
Binder	Guar gum or tragacanth	1/4 tsp	1g	1
Liquid	Water or red wine	4 tsp	17g	16
Aromatic	Valerian root	2 tsp	7.5g	8

Vetiver (Hard to extrude; better for cones)		VOLUME	WEIGHT	RATIO
Base	Sandalwood	1 Tbsp	6g	24
Binder	Guar gum or tragacanth	⅛ tsp	.5g	1
Liquid	Water	4 tsp	17g	32
Aromatic	Vetiver	¾ tsp	2.5g	6

Yohimbe		VOLUME	WEIGHT	RATIO
Base	Red sandalwood	1 Tbsp	4g	24
	Clove	1 tsp	2.5g	8
Binder	Guar gum or tragacanth	⅛ tsp	.5g	1
Liquid	Water	2¾ tsp	13g	22
Aromatic	Yohimbe	½ tsp	.5g	4

Complex Gum Recipes

If you want to use makko instead of a gum binder for these recipes, try substituting makko for both the base material and the binder. Most of the recipes will work well using that method.

Air		VOLUME	WEIGHT	RATIO
Base	Pine	2½ tsp	1.5g	20
	Clove	1 tsp	2.5g	8
Binder	Guar gum or tragacanth	⅛ tsp	.5g	1
Liquid	Water	2 tsp	9.5g	16
Aromatics	Benzoin	½ tsp	2g	4
	Oak moss	½ tsp	.5g	4
	Sage	1 tsp	1g	8

Altars of Fire

		VOLUME	WEIGHT	RATIO
Base	Red cedar	2 tsp	1.5g	16
	Clove	2 tsp	5g	16
Binder	Guar gum or tragacanth	1/8 tsp	.5g	1
Liquid	Water	1 Tbsp	13.5g	24
Aromatics	Myrrh	1/2 tsp	1g	4
	Frankincense	1 tsp	2g	8
	Cinnamon	1/2 tsp	1.5g	4
	Bay	1/2 tsp	1g	4

American Journey

		VOLUME	WEIGHT	RATIO
Base	Pine	2 tsp	1.5g	16
	Clove	1 tsp	2.5g	8
Binder	Guar gum or tragacanth	1/8 tsp	.5g	1
Liquid	Water	2 1/2 tsp	12.5g	20
Aromatics	Cedar (tips)	1/4 tsp	.5g	2
	Coltsfoot	1/2 tsp	.5g	4
	Sage	1/2 tsp	.5g	4

Business Blessings

		VOLUME	WEIGHT	RATIO
Base	Sandalwood	2 1/2 tsp	5g	20
Binder	Guar gum or tragacanth	1/8 tsp	.5g	1
Liquid	Water	4 tsp	17g	32
Aromatics	Bay	1/2 tsp	1g	4
	Benzoin	1/4 tsp	1g	2
	Cinnamon	1/2 tsp	1.5g	4
	Goldenseal	1/4 tsp	.5g	2
	Irish moss	1/4 tsp	.5g	2

Eternal Love (Handfasting)

		VOLUME	WEIGHT	RATIO
Base	Sandalwood	1 Tbsp	6g	24
Binder	Guar gum or tragacanth	1/8 tsp	.5g	1
Liquid	Water	1 Tbsp	13.5g	24
Aromatics	Spikenard	1/2 tsp	.5g	4
	Myrtle	1/2 tsp	1g	4
	Yohimbe	1/4 tsp	<.5g	2

Fertility Rites

		VOLUME	WEIGHT	RATIO
Base	Sandalwood	2 tsp	4g	16
Binder	Guar gum or tragacanth	1/8 tsp	.5g	1
Liquid	Water	2 1/2 tsp	12.5g	20
Aromatics	Myrtle	1/2 tsp	1g	4
	Patchouli	1/4 tsp	.5g	2
	Spikenard	1/2 tsp	.5g	4

Fires of Day

		VOLUME	WEIGHT	RATIO
Base	Red sandalwood	2 tsp	2.5g	16
	Clove	1/2 tsp	1.5g	4
Binder	Guar gum or tragacanth	1/8 tsp	.5g	1
Liquid	Water	2 3/4 tsp	13g	22
Aromatics	Copal	1/4 tsp	.5g	2
	Frankincense	1/4 tsp	.5g	2
	Allspice	1/2 tsp	1g	4
	Galangal	1/4 tsp	.5g	2

Fires of Night

		VOLUME	WEIGHT	RATIO
Base	Red sandalwood	1 Tbsp	4g	24
	Clove	¼ tsp	.5g	2
Binder	Guar gum or tragacanth	⅛ tsp	.5g	1
Liquid	Water	3¼ tsp	15g	26
Aromatics	Cinnamon (cassia)	½ tsp	1.5g	4
	Dragon's blood	½ tsp	1g	4
	Frankincense	½ tsp	1g	4

Fire Water

		VOLUME	WEIGHT	RATIO
Base	Sandalwood	2½ tsp	5g	20
	Clove	¼ tsp	.5g	2
Binder	Guar gum or tragacanth	⅛ tsp	.5g	1
Liquid	Water	1 Tbsp	13.5g	24
Aromatics	Eucalyptus	¼ tsp	.5g	2
	Catnip	½ tsp	1g	4
	Dragon's blood	¼ tsp	.5g	2
	Pennyroyal	½ tsp	.5g	4

Four Quarters (Altar)

		VOLUME	WEIGHT	RATIO
Base	Red sandalwood	2 Tbsp	7.5g	24
	Clove	½ tsp	1.5g	2
Binder	Guar gum or tragacanth	¼ tsp	1g	1
Liquid	Water	3½ tsp	16g	10
Aromatics	Myrrh	½ tsp	1g	2
	Patchouli	1 tsp	1.5g	4
	Copal	1 tsp	2.5g	4

Give Me Strength

		VOLUME	WEIGHT	RATIO
Base	Sandalwood	2 tsp	4g	16
	Clove	½ tsp	1.5g	8
Binder	Guar gum or tragacanth	⅛ tsp	.5g	1
Liquid	Water	2 tsp	9.5g	16
Aromatics	Mugwort	½ tsp	.5g	4
	Pennyroyal	¼ tsp	.5g	2
	Saffron	⅛ tsp	<.5g	1
	Tarragon	⅛ tsp	<.5g	1

Handfasting

		VOLUME	WEIGHT	RATIO
Base	Red sandalwood	4 tsp	5.5g	16
	Benzoin	½ tsp	2g	2
Binder	Guar gum or tragacanth	¼ tsp	1g	1
Liquid	White wine	5 tsp	20.5g	20
Aromatics	Bay leaf	½ tsp	1g	2
	Cinnamon	½ tsp	1.5g	2
	Patchouli	½ tsp	1g	2
	Yohimbe root	½ tsp	.5g	2

Happy Cats

		VOLUME	WEIGHT	RATIO
Base	Sandalwood	2 tsp	4g	16
Binder	Guar gum or tragacanth	⅛ tsp	.5g	1
Liquid	Water	1 Tbsp	13.5g	24
Aromatics	Catnip	½ tsp	1g	4
	Palo santo	1 tsp	1g	8

79

Incan Sunrise

		VOLUME	WEIGHT	RATIO
Base	Red cedar	2 tsp	1.5g	16
	Clove	1/2 tsp	1.5g	4
Binder	Guar gum or tragacanth	1/8 tsp	.5g	1
Liquid	Water	2 tsp	9.5g	16
Aromatics	Black copal	1/4 tsp	.5g	2
	Palo santo	1/4 tsp	<.5g	2
	Tonka bean skin	1/8 tsp	<.5g	1
	White copal	1/4 tsp	.5g	2

Juniper

		VOLUME	WEIGHT	RATIO
Base	Sandalwood	2 tsp	4g	16
Binder	Guar gum or tragacanth	1/8 tsp	.5g	1
Liquid	Water	2 1/2 tsp	12.5g	20
Aromatics	Juniper tips	1 tsp	1g	8
	Juniper berry	1 tsp	1.5g	8

Lair of the Dragon

		VOLUME	WEIGHT	RATIO
Base	Red sandalwood	2 Tbsp	7.5g	24
	Clove	1 tsp	2.5g	4
Binder	Guar gum or tragacanth	1/4 tsp	1g	1
Liquid	Water or red wine	7 tsp	30.5g	28
Aromatics	Dragon's blood	3/4 tsp	1.5g	3
	Tarragon	1/4 tsp	.5g	1
	Frankincense	1 tsp	2g	4
	Benzoin	1/2 tsp	2g	2
	Turmeric	1/2 tsp	1g	2
	Cinnamon	1/2 tsp	1.5g	2

Luck

Base		VOLUME	WEIGHT	RATIO
Base	Pine	1 Tbsp	2g	24
	Clove	1 tsp	2.5g	8
Binder	Guar gum or tragacanth	1/8 tsp	.5g	1
Liquid	Water	2 1/2 tsp	12.5g	20
Aromatics	Calamus	1/4 tsp	.5g	2
	Star anise	1/2 tsp	.5g	4
	Oak moss	1/4 tsp	<.5g	2

Mist

		VOLUME	WEIGHT	RATIO
Base	Sandalwood	1 tsp	2g	8
	Red sandalwood	1 tsp	1.5g	8
	Clove	1/2 tsp	1.5g	4
Binder	Guar gum or tragacanth	1/8 tsp	.5g	1
Liquid	Water	1 Tbsp	13.5g	24
Aromatics	White willow	1/2 tsp	1g	4
	Horehound	1/2 tsp	.5g	4
	Frankincense	1/2 tsp	1g	4

Occidental

		VOLUME	WEIGHT	RATIO
Base	Red cedar	2 Tbsp	7.5g	24
Binder	Guar gum or tragacanth	1/4 tsp	1g	1
Liquid	Water	7 tsp	30.5g	28
Aromatics	Allspice	1/2 tsp	1g	2
	Copal	1/2 tsp	1.5g	2
	Rosemary	1/2 tsp	.5g	2
	Woodruff	1/2 tsp	.5g	2

Sanctification

		VOLUME	WEIGHT	RATIO
Base	Red cedar	1 Tbsp	2.5g	24
	Clove	1/2 tsp	1.5g	4
Binder	Guar gum or tragacanth	1/8 tsp	.5g	1
Liquid	Water	2 3/4 tsp	13g	22
Aromatics	Valerian	1/8 tsp	<.5g	1
	Star anise	1 tsp	1.5g	8
	Rosemary	1/2 tsp	.5g	4
	Ginger	1/4 tsp	.5g	2
	Eucalyptus	1/2 tsp	1g	4

82

Scarborough Faire

		VOLUME	WEIGHT	RATIO
Base	Pine	2 tsp	1.5g	16
	Clove	1 tsp	2.5g	8
Binder	Guar gum or tragacanth	1/8 tsp	.5g	1
Liquid	Water	2 1/2 tsp	12.5g	20
Aromatics	Parsley	1/8 tsp	<.5g	1
	Sage	1 tsp	1g	8
	Rosemary	1/4 tsp	<.5g	2
	Thyme	1/2 tsp	.5g	4

Small World

		VOLUME	WEIGHT	RATIO
Base	Sandalwood	2 Tbsp	7.5g	24
Binder	Guar gum or tragacanth	1/4 tsp	1g	1
Liquid	Water or wine	4 tsp	17g	16
Aromatics	Chamomile	1 tsp	1g	4
	Lemon grass	1 tsp	1.5g	4
	Palo santo	1 tsp	1g	4

To the One I Love

		VOLUME	WEIGHT	RATIO
Base	Red sandalwood	1 Tbsp	4g	24
	Clove	½ tsp	1.5g	4
Binder	Guar gum or tragacanth	⅛ tsp	.5g	1
Liquid	Water	3¼ tsp	15g	26
Aromatics	Cardamom	¼ tsp	.5g	2
	Lavender	¾ tsp	.5g	6
	Marjoram	½ tsp	.5g	4
	Myrtle	½ tsp	1g	4

Water

		VOLUME	WEIGHT	RATIO
Base	Sandalwood	2 tsp	4g	16
	Clove	½ tsp	1.5g	4
Binder	Guar gum or tragacanth	⅛ tsp	.5g	1
Liquid	Water	1 Tbsp	13.5g	24
Aromatics	Calamus	½ tsp	1g	4
	Myrrh	½ tsp	1g	4
	White willow bark	¼ tsp	.5g	2

Visions of Love

		VOLUME	WEIGHT	RATIO
Base	Sandalwood	2 tsp	4g	16
	Clove	½ tsp	1.5g	4
Binder	Guar gum or tragacanth	⅛ tsp	.5g	1
Liquid	Water	2¾ tsp	13g	22
Aromatics	Chamomile	¼ tsp	.5g	2
	Coltsfoot	½ tsp	<.5g	2
	Damiana	1 tsp	1.5g	8
	Hibiscus	¼ tsp	.5g	2
	Yohimbe	¼ tsp	<.5g	2

Complex Makko Recipes

If you want to use guar gum or tragacanth instead of makko in these recipes, here's a good tip. Use ⅛ teaspoon of gum binder, then add sandalwood in place of the makko. Remember to subtract ⅛ teaspoon from the total amount of makko. That will work for many of these recipes.

Cleansing

		VOLUME	WEIGHT	RATIO
Base	Makko	2 tsp	3g	8
Liquid	Water	2¼ tsp	11g	9
Aromatics	Bay	1 tsp	2g	4
	Benzoin	½ tsp	2g	2
	Frankincense	½ tsp	1g	2

Earth

		VOLUME	WEIGHT	RATIO
Base	Makko	2 tsp	3g	8
	Clove	¼ tsp	.5g	1
Liquid	Water	1 Tbsp	13.5g	12
Aromatics	Patchouli	1 tsp	1.5g	4
	Wild lettuce	½ tsp	.5g	2
	Yohimbe	½ tsp	.5g	2

Japan

		VOLUME	WEIGHT	RATIO
Base	Sandalwood	2 tsp	4g	8
	Clove	1 tsp	2.5g	4
Binder	Makko	2 tsp	3g	8
Liquid	Water	4¼ tsp	18g	17
Aromatics	Cinnamon	½ tsp	1.5g	2
	Star anise	½ tsp	.5g	2

Mourning		VOLUME	WEIGHT	RATIO
Base	Sandalwood	1 Tbsp	6g	12
Binder	Makko	1 tsp	1.5g	4
	Clove	½ tsp	1.5g	2
Liquid	Water	1 Tbsp	13.5g	12
Aromatics	Lemon grass	¼ tsp	.5g	1
	Lavender	¼ tsp	<.5g	1
	Myrrh	¼ tsp	.5g	1
	Palo santo	¼ tsp	<.5g	1

Moist Incense Recipes

Just as you want to add the minimum amount of water in a self-burning incense, for moist incense (which has to be burned over charcoal) you want to add the least amount of binder possible. These recipes use honey as the binder, so add the least amount possible. The amount of honey in the recipe is only a rough guideline, so use your judgment as you add it to the blend. Add enough to hold the incense together in a single ball, but add no more than that. After adding more binder, knead the dough thoroughly. A little goes a long way.

Most of the recipes include powdered charcoal. Be certain that you use high-quality charcoal and not the self-lighting type. Even if you burn your moist incense on self-lighting charcoal you should use only high-quality charcoal as an ingredient. Self-lighting charcoal included in your recipe will cause the incense to smell bad and burn too hot and too fast.

Once you have mixed in the honey, you can either roll the incense into pea-sized balls or you can leave the dough in a single piece. You should seal it in an air-tight container (such as a jar) and allow it to age for several weeks. Keep it out of the light and away from excessive heat. Once it has aged you can burn the balls you rolled or simply roll them as you need them.

5-4-3-2-1 Nerikoh

		VOLUME	WEIGHT	RATIO
Base	Sandalwood	1¼ tsp	2.5g	5
	Clove	1 tsp	2.5g	4
Binder	Honey (as needed)	1 tsp	6g	4
Aromatics	Cinnamon (cassia)	¾ tsp	2g	3
	Star anise	½ tsp	.5g	2
	Benzoin	¼ tsp	1g	1

Cleansing Love

		VOLUME	WEIGHT	RATIO
Base	Sandalwood	2 tsp	4g	8
	Charcoal	¼ tsp	.5g	1
	Benzoin	½ tsp	2g	2
Binder	Honey (as needed)	2¼ tsp	14.5g	10
Aromatics	Chamomile	½ tsp	1g	2
	Copal	¼ tsp	.5g	1
	Lavender	½ tsp	.5g	2

Parting of Old Friends

		VOLUME	WEIGHT	RATIO
Base	Sandalwood	2 tsp	4g	8
	Clove	1 tsp	2.5g	4
	Charcoal	¼ tsp	.5g	1
	Benzoin	¼ tsp	1g	1
Binder	Honey (as needed)	2¼ tsp	14.5g	9
Aromatics	Hyssop	½ tsp	.5g	2
	Juniper berry	¼ tsp	<.5g	1
	Lemon grass	¼ tsp	.5g	1
	Myrtle	½ tsp	1g	2

Protection

		VOLUME	WEIGHT	RATIO
Base	Pine	2 tsp	1.5g	8
	Clove	1 tsp	2.5g	4
	Benzoin	¼ tsp	1g	1
Binder	Honey (as needed)	1¼ tsp	8g	5
Aromatics	Dragon's blood	¼ tsp	.5g	1
	Frankincense	¼ tsp	.5g	1
	Horehound	¼ tsp	<.5g	1
	Marjoram	½ tsp	.5g	2

Purity

		VOLUME	WEIGHT	RATIO
Base	Red cedar	2 tsp	1.5g	8
	Clove	¾ tsp	2g	3
	Charcoal	½ tsp	1g	2
	Benzoin	¼ tsp	1g	1
Binder	Honey (as needed)	1½ tsp	9.5g	6
Aromatics	Oak moss	½ tsp	.5g	2
	Rosemary	½ tsp	.5g	2

Strength

		VOLUME	WEIGHT	RATIO
Base	Red cedar	1½ tsp	1g	6
	Charcoal	½ tsp	1g	2
	Benzoin	¼ tsp	1g	1
Binder	Honey (as needed)	1 tsp	6g	4
Aromatics	Palo santo	¼ tsp	<.5g	1
	Saffron	Dash	<.5g	Dash
	Tarragon	½ tsp	1g	2

True Love

		VOLUME	WEIGHT	RATIO
Base	Red sandalwood	2 tsp	2.5g	8
	Clove	1 tsp	2.5g	4
	Charcoal	1/4 tsp	.5g	1
Binder	Honey (as needed)	2 tsp	13.5g	8
Aromatics	Cardamom	1/4 tsp	.5g	1
	Ginger	1/4 tsp	.5g	1
	Hibiscus	1/2 tsp	1.5g	2
	Valerian	1/4 tsp	.5g	1
	White willow	1/2 tsp	1g	2

Twilight

		VOLUME	WEIGHT	RATIO
Base	Sandalwood	2 tsp	4g	8
	Clove	1/2 tsp	1.5g	2
	Charcoal	1/2 tsp	1g	2
	Benzoin	1/4 tsp	1g	1
Binder	Honey (as needed)	1 3/4 tsp	11.5g	7
Aromatics	Bay	1/4 tsp	.5g	1
	Cardamom	1/4 tsp	.5g	1
	Frankincense	1/2 tsp	1g	2

Victory

		Volume	Weight	Ratio
Base	Sandalwood	2¼ tsp	4.5g	9
	Clove	½ tsp	1.5g	2
	Charcoal	½ tsp	1g	2
	Benzoin	¼ tsp	1g	1
Binder	Honey (as needed)	2½ tsp	16g	10
Aromatics	Oak moss	½ tsp	.5g	2
	Tarragon	¼ tsp	.5g	1
	Woodruff	½ tsp	.5g	2

CHAPTER EIGHT

EXPERIMENTATION

ALTHOUGH DOGMA MAKES some incense makers oppose experimentation, it can be the most pleasurable aspect of the incense-making process. Creating a new combination of aromatics can not only be fun, but pleasantly surprising when you create something new that's never been experienced before. Beyond that, experimentation is the only way that you can incorporate a new ingredient into your incense. You will not find books and preprinted incense recipes that list every conceivable ingredient or combinations of ingredients, so experimenting is the only way to use local materials. I truly consider this to be at the heart of great incense.

To a certain degree, all incense making from recipes involves substitution and experimentation. Although you might follow my recipe precisely, unless you have gotten all of your ingredients from the same batch that I used, your incense will smell a bit different than mine. The purpose of a recipe isn't to duplicate the precise smell of someone else's incense. Rather, recipes are a way to suggest combinations that should yield pleasant results regardless of differences in scent. Even using two identical species of plant can yield different results if they were grown in different places.

Substitutions

Inevitably, you will find a recipe that you want to try but lack one ingredient. That is especially a problem for new incense makers who haven't built up their cupboard to include a wide variety of ingredients. Often you can find a reasonable substitute among your supplies. There are a few simple things to keep in mind when selecting substitutes.

First, always replace an ingredient with another of the same type. If you need to substitute for a resin, use another resin. Replace one kind of wood with a different wood. Use one flower as a substitute for another. This will help to keep the same burning characteristics in the incense. Second, seek similar scents when possible. Copal smells similar to frankincense. Oak moss and Irish moss are similar. Of course, the nice thing about aromatics is that they are all unique, but that makes substitutions both very difficult (if you want to imitate the exact scent of another batch of incense) and very easy (since different batches of the same ingredient vary, all incense making is substitution in a sense). Finally, when making magick incense, you need to use substitutes with similar magickal properties. Especially watch the elemental sign of the substitute. For example, you might not want to replace an aromatic that is under the sign of Water with one under the sign of Fire.

New Blends

The creation of new blends is the most rewarding aspect of incense making. Carefully blending a new combination of aromatics and bases is exciting, but as with all incense making, it requires patience. Testing is an important first step.

Testing

Rolling a batch of incense can involve using up materials that you might not have in abundance. As well, rolling a batch of incense is a big time commitment. Not so much in the actual rolling of the incense (which goes by all too quickly) but in the drying time. It might take you four days to find out that your new blend is less than pleasing. That's why testing is so important.

After deciding on your new blend you really need to confirm that the scent meets your expectations. The only practical way to test your blend is to burn it. This is why all incense makers need to keep some high-quality charcoal on hand. Light your charcoal and place it in a censer filled with sand or ash when you're ready to test. Be warned that using "self-lighting" incense will cause some distortion of the scent due to its saltpeter content.

Begin by mixing the aromatic ingredients. Don't mix very much, just small amounts until you have the scent you desire. Sprinkle a small amount of this mixture onto your burning charcoal. If the smell isn't what you want you can easily adjust it at this stage. You might have to repeat this procedure many times to find the exact scent or effect that you want. If you have a very specific aroma in mind it might take you weeks or months to find the right ingredients.

Once you've achieved the correct blend of aromatics, it's time to add some base material. Experience will teach you how much to add as you make more and more incense, but for early experimentation I would suggest that you add one part aromatic to four parts base material. Test that mixture on your charcoal first. If you find the smell to be too "muted" or altered by the base, you can gradually reduce the ratio of base material until you find a scent that pleases you. Once you're happy with the scent you can add some binder to your mixture and you're ready to roll incense. Be careful not to add more binder than needed. Start with a tiny bit and add more if you find the incense won't hold together. Once you've rolled a batch and dried it, you can test its burning properties. If you find the incense burns and then goes out, you might try increasing the amount of base material or adding clove powder to your mixture. You should also consult the troubleshooting chart in chapter 9.

You might consider experimenting by taking an existing recipe and modifying it. The easiest way to do that is by substituting a different ingredient for one in the recipe. If your desire is to experiment with new blends then you should throw out the guide that I offered earlier. Rather than trying to imitate an ingredient you don't have on hand, try replacing one ingredient with one that is radically different. If the recipe calls for patchouli, try saffron instead. If it calls for copal, try oregano instead.

Patience

As with most other aspects of incense making, creating new blends that work well and give the desired effect requires patience. You might have to test many recipes to find the right one. You might have to seek out a new ingredient in order to achieve the exact scent that you desire. This is part of the fun of experimenting. It might take you years to perfect a favorite recipe, but the journey is half the joy of the project. It may require a lot of experimentation to create a blend that burns well as a stick or cone and produces the right scent. Remember that some secret incense recipes were developed over hundreds of years—don't get discouraged if your first experiments aren't perfect.

Aging

A final factor to keep in mind is aging. You will get the best results from any incense you make by allowing your powdered ingredients (aside from gum binders) to sit together and age before rolling or even testing. Unless you roll the incense and use it right away, it will age on your shelf while awaiting use so it's wise to test an aged blend. Even aging for a week or two can create a much more complete blending of scents than powder mixed and burned immediately. For best results you should age all your powdered blends for three months before use, although I only do this for very special blends.

The Importance of Notetaking

I can't stress enough the importance of taking good notes when you experiment with incense. I can't count the number of incense blends that I've created, modified, and perfected, only to forget how I made them. Don't trust your memory to record your experiments. Write everything down and keep the details of each modified batch you make. It is heartbreaking to burn your final stick of a perfect blend and never be able to recreate the scent again.

Adapting Other Recipes

You might have other incense books on your shelf with recipes that you want to try. Sadly, the bulk of incense books deal only with loose incense. You can still adapt these recipes for use in self-burning incense. Keep in mind that, unlike loose incense, rolled incense needs to be completely powdered. Powder all of the ingredients in the given loose incense recipe and carefully sift it. Then you will need to add a base material. The amount that you need will depend on the burning properties of the aromatics in the recipes. If you are using weak-scented ingredients that burn well (lavender is a good example) you won't need to add much base material. If, on the other hand, you're using aromatics that are hard to burn or that have a very strong scent (myrrh qualifies in both categories) then you will need to use far more base material.

If you're uncertain how much base to start with, I'd suggest a ratio of one part aromatic blend to four parts base material. You also need to give some consideration to the base you plan to use. The primary consideration is, naturally, what materials you have available to you. If you only have one base material in your cupboard then you'll need to use it. If you

94

have more than one base available, open your containers and smell the various bases you have. Does one seem more complementary than the others? If so, use that one. If scent won't tell you which to use, you might consider color. How incense looks is also part of its appeal. If you're making a blend with a lot of cinnamon, you might want to use red cedar or red sandalwood as your base since the colors are complementary. Finally, if you're using aromatics that are difficult to burn or that you're unsure about, you should add a small amount of clove to your base. If you later find that the blend burns well or too fast you can reduce the amount of clove in future batches.

95

You might also encounter recipes in some books that call for the use of saltpeter. You should certainly disregard that idea. Instead, either increase the amount of base material or the amount of clove in the base. Both of those options will improve the burning properties of your incense, although they might also impact the scent slightly.

Experimenting with incense is both fun and rewarding, although it can test your patience at times. Whether you are simply looking for substitutions for ingredients you can't locate or are trying to create something completely new, experimentation demands good note taking. Don't ruin all your work by failing to record how you did it. Should that ever happen to you, enjoy the incense while it's there and remember it once it's gone. Test your blends and take your time in perfecting your recipes. You will be rewarded with incense that is unequaled.

CHAPTER NINE

TROUBLESHOOTING

EVENTUALLY, ALL INCENSE makers create incense that doesn't burn well (or perhaps not at all). Use the following chart as a guide to help you with any problems you might have. I certainly can't offer the solution to every problem since your ingredients will be a unique combination of materials. Nevertheless, this chart will give you some valuable suggestions for correcting the problem.

To use the chart, look in the first column until you find the problem most closely matching your own. Once you locate the problem, look across the chart to the second column. If there is a question in that column, read it and then find the bold answer in the third column. If there is no question in the second column, skip over to the third column. Each row gives you a different suggested solution. Some only offer one suggestion, while some offer many.

If all else fails, you can always grind the incense back to powder and add more base material and roll again. If you don't want to go to that trouble, and you have incense that won't burn, you can also burn it on charcoal or throw it into your next campfire.

Problem	Question	Possible Solutions
Dry mix has lumps in the powder		Break the lumps up with your mixing stick and stir further.
Dry mix has hard lumps that won't stir together		You need to screen your ingredients again. Too many large particles are in your mix.
Dough won't stick together	Is it moist?	**No**—add another ¼ tsp water and mix again **Yes**—sprinkle with a very tiny amount of binder and mix again
Dough stiff and cracked		Add another ¼ tsp water and knead further You may have used too little binder. Add a dash of binder and water as needed.
Dough droops and sags	Did you use makko as your binder?	**No**—You have added too much liquid. You can add more base material or you can allow the dough to sit for 15 minutes so it can dry out. **Yes**—Makko will dry out given time, but for quickest results add another ¼ tsp of makko and knead again for several minutes. This step should be repeated until the dough is the proper consistency.
Dough sticks to hands and tools	Did you use makko or gum arabic as your binder?	**Yes**—These binders tend to be sticky. To minimize this, use colder water and use as little binder as possible. Try refrigerating your dough before handling it. **No**—You have probably used too much binder. Add more base

Problem	Question	Possible Solutions
		material (and more aromatics if needed) and continue to knead.
Dough is difficult to extrude	Is the extruder becoming plugged?	**Yes**—You didn't screen your ingredients well enough before use. Clean out any large particles in the dough. Screen the dry ingredients before using them again.
	Are you using makko as your binder?	**Yes**—You may need to add additional makko to help the dough flow better.
	Are you using gum arabic as your binder?	**Yes**—Gum arabic does not do well in an extruder. Roll your incense by hand instead.
		No—Add $1/4$ tsp warm or hot water and knead before further extruding.
Dough is difficult to use in a mold	Are you using makko or gum arabic as your binder?	**Yes**—These binders are not well suited for molding. Try using cold water and swab the inside of the mold with water. Luck will also help.
		No—Try molding after thoroughly swabbing the inside of the mold with water.
		If the dough is warm, try cooling it down in the refrigerator for 15 minutes and mold again.
		The dough may be too wet. Add another $1/2$ tsp base material, knead, and mold again.
		You may need to add more binder to your mixture. Do this with great care and add less than $1/8$ tsp of binder.

99

Problem	Question	Possible Solutions
Cones lose their shape while drying		You have used too much water. Add another ¼ tsp base to your dough, knead, and roll the cone again. You can also allow the dough to dry for 10 minutes before rolling again.
Cones tip over while drying or after dried		The cone was most likely set down at an angle. Carefully check each wet cone after you've put it on your drying board to make certain it is standing up straight.
Cone bottoms are flared		This happens as you press the cone down. Try cutting the bottom with a hobby knife instead.
Sticks or coils curl up when dry	Did you dry them slowly?	**Yes**—You may have used too much binder. Also keep in mind that most gum binders will tend to deform a bit as they dry, so a little curling might be inevitable with the binder you're using. Don't turn or move your stick or coil incense until it has had time to completely dry. Changing its position before it has finished drying can amplify curling. **No**—Always dry your incense slowly. Trying to accelerate the process can cause your incense to warp.
Incense cones break apart when dried		You need more binder in your recipe. Grind up the cones and add more binder before rolling again. Or handle with care and burn them anyway.

Problem	Question	Possible Solutions
Incense sticks break too easily when dried		You may need to reduce the amount of aromatic in your blend (or increase the amount of base material). Mixes with a lot of resins or plant material can sometimes be soft.
Smoke comes out the bottom or side of incense while burning		The incense is cracked. You might be able to see the cracks, you might not. If this has happened the incense might go out while burning. The most likely cause for this is rapid drying. Dry your incense slowly. Another likely cause is too much water in the dough. Try making it with less water. The cracking might be caused by using too little binder. Increase the amount of binder very gradually. You might need to increase the amount of base material in your blend.
Incense won't burn or goes out multiple times	Has it been more than three days since the incense was rolled?	**No**—Let the incense continue to dry. I know it's hard to wait, but the incense needs to dry untouched. You might need to reduce the amount of aromatic material in your recipe or increase the amount of base material. Try the other suggestions in this chart first, then reformulate the incense if you need to.

Problem	Question	Possible Solutions
	Is the incense dry?	**No**—If the incense is darker on one side than the other or if it is pliable then it may not be dry despite the number of days it has been sitting there. Allow another 48 hours and check again to see if it's dry.
	Are you trying to burn cone incense?	**Yes**—Your cones may be too large. The fattest part of the cone should be no wider than an unsharpened pencil. This is probably the case if the cones burn more than halfway down.
		You may have used too much binder. This is likely if the cones are dry but go out shortly after being lit. Another sign of too much binder is if you see that the ash on the cone has a considerably smaller diameter than the unburned cone below it (a "pulled-in" look to the ash). If you see that, you probably need to reduce the amount of binder in your blend. If the ashes from the incense stick together extremely well you may have used too much binder.
		Trying rolling some of your blend into a spaghetti stick. If the spaghetti stick burns but the cone won't, you should increase the amount of base in your blend and try the cones again. Alternately, you can just roll spaghetti sticks instead of cones.

Problem	Question	Possible Solutions
		If your blend still won't burn, you have too many hard-to-burn materials in your formula. Cut the amount of aromatic plant materials in half and try the blend again. Make certain that all the ingredients in your blend are properly dried before mixing. You may need to start over with a new recipe.
	Are you trying to burn sticks with bamboo rods?	**Yes**—First, ask yourself: "Does this stick really need to be here?" Unless you plan to ship your incense around the world, a bamboo rod isn't really a good form to use. The rod itself can often keep the incense from burning. Try the toothpick method instead. Is the incense cracked on the rod? If bits fall off or smoke comes out of cracks in the incense, read the suggestions for cracking. The incense may not be firmly pressed together on the stick. Make certain to apply firm and even pressure to all parts of the stick to ensure that it holds well to the rod.

Appendix A:

Ingredients Chart

THE FOLLOWING CHART is by no means comprehensive. There are hundreds of incense-making ingredients, and it would fill an entire book just to list them all. However, this should provide you with some basic information to choose ingredients.

For more complete information about these and other ingredients, consult a good reference book such as *Cunningham's Encyclopedia of Magical Herbs* (Llewellyn Publications, 1985), which will offer you far more detail.

Common Name	Latin Name	Category	Base	Binder	Aromatic	Elemental Association	Traditional Associations	Notes
Allspice	*Eugenia pementa*	plant			●	Fire	money, prosperity, wisdom	
Anise (seed)	*Pimpinella anisum*	plant			●	Air	cleansing, youth	
Bay leaf (laurel)	*Laurus nobilis*	plant			●	Fire	protection healing, cleansing	
Benzoin gum*	*Styrax benzoin*	resin	●		●	Air	cleansing, prosperity	* When used as a base material, benzoin serves mainly as a fixative to help preserve and blend the scent, and is especially useful in recipes that use oils.
Calamus (root)	*Acorus calamus*	plant			●	Water	luck, healing, money, protection	
Cardamom	*Ellettrua cardamomum*	plant			●	Water	love, care	
Catnip*	*Nepeta cataria*	plant			●	Water	felines, love, beauty, happiness	* Take care when using catnip in your blends. Keep drying incense well out of the reach of cats.

106

Common Name	Latin Name	Category	Base	Binder	Aromatic	Elemental Association	Traditional Associations	Notes
Cedar	Cedrus spp.	wood	●		●	Fire	Healing, purification, protection	
Chamomile	Matricaria chamomilla	plant			●	Water	Sleep, love, cleansing	
Cinnamon (cassia)*	Cinnamomum cassia	wood			●	Fire	Success, healing, power, protection	* This is properly called "cassia," but in the U.S. most products labeled "cinnamon" are actually cassia. Cassia should be used in incense as true cinnamon won't give as good a result.
Clove*	Carophyllus aramaticus	plant	●		●	Fire	Protection, exorcism, love	
Coltsfoot*	Tussilago farfara	plant			●	Water	Visions, love	
Copal*	Bursera odorata	resin			●	Fire	Love, cleansing	* Clove is an important addition to your base to help blends that won't burn or that burn and go out.
Costus (root)	Sassurea lappa	plant			●	Water	Love, rejuvenation	
Damiana*	Turnera aphrodisiaca	plant			●	Fire	Love, visions	* Coltsfoot may cause psychotropic effects.
Dragon's blood	Calamus draco	resin			●	Fire	Love, protection, exorcism, potency	* Copal is available in black, white, and golden forms.
Eucalyptus	Eucalyptus globules	plant			●	Water	Healing, protection	
Frankincense	Boswellia serrata	resin			●	Fire	Protection, summoning, cleansing	* Damiana may cause psychotropic effects.
Galangal (root)	Alpina officinalis	plant			●	Fire	Protection, health, money, hex-breaking	
Ginger (root)	Zingiber officinate	plant			●	Fire	Love, success, power	
Goldenseal (root)	Hydrastis canadensis	plant			●	Fire	Money, healing	
Gum arabic (acacia)	Acacia senegal	plant		●		Air	Protection	
Guar gum	Cyamopsis tetragonolobus	plant		●		Fire	Devotion	
Hibiscus	Hibiscus rosasinensis	plant			●	Water	Love, lust, divination	
Horehound	Marrubium vulgare	plant			●	Air	Protection, mental powers, healing	
Hops (flower)*	Humulus lupulus	plant			●	Air	Sleep, visions	* Hops may cause psychotropic effects.

Common Name	Latin Name	Category	Base	Binder	Aromatic	Elemental Association	Traditional Associations	Notes
Hyssop	*Hyssopus officinalis*	plant			●	Fire	Purification, protection, sanctification	
Irish moss	*Chrondus crispus*	plant			●	Water	Money, luck	
Juniper (berry)	*Juniperus communis*	plant			●	Fire	Protection, health, sanctification	
Juniper (wood and needles)	*Juniperus communis*	wood	●		●	Fire	Protection, health, sanctification	
Lavender (flowers)	*Lavandula officinalis*	plant			●	Air	Love, protection, sleep, cleansing	
Lemon grass*	*Cymbopogon citrates*	plant			●	Air	Separation, purity	* Although some incense books have listed this ingredient as poisonous, that is not true. It is used in cooking, so I'd ignore those others who fear it.
Makko (tabu)	*Machillus thunbergii*	wood	●	●		Earth	Cleansing, truth	
Marjoram	*Origanum marjorana*	plant			●	Air	Love, happiness, protection	
Mugwort	*Artemisia vulgaris*	plant			●	Earth	Strength, divination, healing	
Myrrh	*Commiphora molmol*	resin			●	Water	Protection, healing, spirituality	
Myrtle (leaf)	*Myrtus communis*	plant			●	Water	Fertility, love, long life	
Oak moss	*Evernia prunastri*	plant	●		●	Air	Luck, money	
Palo santo*	*Bursera graveolens*	wood			●	Air	Cleansing, luck, strength	* The scent of this wood is so strong that I wouldn't use it as a base material, although you could.
Parsley (leaf)	*Petroselinum sativum*	plant			●	Air	Protection, cleansing, fertility	
Patchouli (leaf)	*Pogosemon patchouly*	plant			●	Earth	Money, fertility, lust	
Pennyroyal	*Mentha pulegium*	plant			●	Fire	Strength, protection, peace	
Pine	*Pinus spp.*	wood	●		●	Air	Healing, fertility, protection	
Red cedar	*Juniperus virginiana*	wood	●			Earth	Strength, honor, honesty	

108

COMMON NAME	LATIN NAME	CATEGORY	BASE	BINDER	AROMATIC	ELEMENTAL ASSOCIATION	TRADITIONAL ASSOCIATIONS	NOTES
Rosemary	*Rosmarnius officinalis*	plant			●	Fire	Sleep, healing, cleansing	
Saffron	*Crocus sativus*	plant			●	Fire	Love, strength, happiness	
Sage (leaf)	*Salvia officinalis*	plant			●	Air	Immortality, longevity, wishes	
Sandalwood (yellow)*	*Santalum album*	wood	●		●	Water	Wishes, healing, spirituality	* Indian yellow sandalwood is an endangered species, so you might want to avoid using it.
Sandalwood (red)	*Pterocarpus santalinus*	wood	●		●	Air	Cleansing, revelation	
Spikenard	*Aralia racemosa*	plant			●	Water	Health, fidelity	
Star anise	*Illicium anisatum*	plant			●	Air	Luck, power	
Tarragon (leaf)	*Artemisia dracunculus*	plant			●	Fire	Strength, courage	
Thyme (leaf)	*Thymus vulgaris*	plant			●	Water	Health, sleep, courage	
Tonka (bean)	*Dipteryx odorato*	plant			●	Water	Courage, wishes, love	
Tragacanth gum	*Astragalus*	plant		●		Water	Binding	
Turmeric	*Cucurma longa*	plant			●	Fire	Purification	
Valerian (root)	*Valeriana officinalis*	plant			●	Water	Sleep, cleansing, love	
Vetiver (root)	*Vetiveria zizanioides*	plant			●	Earth	Luck, money, hex-breaking	
White willow (bark)	*Salix alba*	wood	●		●	Water	Love, divination, healing	
Wild lettuce*	*Latuca virosa*	plant			●	Earth	Divination, visions, revelation	* Wild lettuce may cause psychotropic effects.
Woodruff	*Asperula odorata*	plant			●	Fire	Victory, protection	
Yohimbe (root)	*Corynanthe yohimbe*	plant			●	Earth	Love, lust, desire	

Appendix B:

Locating Materials

Perhaps the most challenging part of incense making, especially when you begin, is finding the ingredients you need. Luckily, in the twenty-first century we have many sources for incense-making supplies. From your local pet supply store to the Internet, you can find almost any ingredient you could want and have it in your hands in just a few weeks (sometimes in mere minutes).

Local Sources

Many New Age shops and book stores have an herb section. They are an especially good local source if you're lucky enough to have one in your town. Unlike gourmet or herb shops, the New Age shops understand that you might use these materials for incense. They often sell base materials and a wide array of aromatics. Sadly, very few of these shops sell binders. However, they do have access to them, although they might not realize it. If your local New Age shop sells herbs and other aromatics, ask them if they can order binders for you. Although makko isn't easily available to them, guar gum and gum tragacanth are often available from herb suppliers. Gum arabic (acacia) is available from most wholesale herb suppliers. A local shop that will place special orders for you is the greatest source you can ask for. Many people don't have access to one of these wonderful places, but there are still plenty of local alternatives.

If you live in a very large city, you might even be lucky enough to have a Japanese incense shop. I know of a dozen or so such shops across the U.S. and more every year. If your city has one, they might be able to supply you with high-quality aromatics, bases, and hopefully makko (they might call it "tabu") in addition to bamboo charcoal and all the items need for kodo-style incense burning (see Appendix E for more information). Makko has only recently reached the shores of America, but as knowledge of it spreads it will become more available here. Most incense makers (including your author) aren't lucky enough to have one of these shops nearby.

Most new incense makers begin by raiding their kitchen's spice rack. You can certainly do that (I'm sure the first cinnamon I ever used was from my spice rack—sage too I believe), although you'll find a good incense supplier will offer much higher quality aromatics than your grocery store. Even the smallest grocery store will offer a few useful incense-making ingredients. Large grocery stores often have a wide array of spices. In the spice section you might find acacia, which is a binder. It's not very easy to use, but it will work. Check your local phone book for both herb shops and gourmet shops. Call herb shops before visiting to confirm that they sell loose herbs and not just ground herbs in capsules. Gourmet shops often offer an even wider selection of herbs than the largest grocery store. Although you might find some acacia, these sources won't provide you with the binders that really make incense work well.

There are many local sources for base material. I find that red cedar is an acceptable base for incense. You can find red cedar shavings in your local pet supply store (or even in some grocery stores in the pet section) as a bedding material for animals. Be sure to check the package to make certain that the wood hasn't been treated with any chemicals (although it rarely is). The shavings can be ground and sifted to use as a base for incense. Many pet shops also sell pine wood shavings. These are usually easier to powder and will also work well as a base, although they will add a pine scent to any incense made that way. If you are lucky enough to have fruit trees growing nearby, be certain to gather any fallen wood from the trees and any branches that are trimmed away. That wood can be chipped, dried, and then powdered to use as base material. The needles from evergreens can also be used. They can be collected from under trees and from fallen or trimmed branches. They can even be purchased at many garden supply stores where they are sold as mulch.

Finding binders (aside from the low-quality ones you might find in the spice section) is the most difficult task. If you don't have any local shop that will order binders for you, look in your local phone book under "chemical suppliers." Even small cities will have several such businesses. Large cities might have dozens. These suppliers can usually get both guar gum and gum tragacanth. Sometimes they will have them in stock, but often you will have to special order them. Buying from chemical suppliers is usually the most expensive alternative. Often, the chemical suppliers will charge double or triple the price you'd pay elsewhere and they might require you to purchase more than you'd like to. On the other hand, the binders from chemical suppliers are generally of the very highest quality. If you buy binders from a chemical supplier you might find that you can reduce the amount of binder in all the recipes in this book. If you use binders from these suppliers and find that all your incense goes out without burning completely, cut the amount of binder in your recipes by 50 percent.

Mail Order and the Internet

I always feel that you should exhaust your local supplies before ordering from elsewhere. If you can use wood from your own land as a base material, I say use it! Don't let it go to waste and, by the same token, you are producing a more unique product based on your local ecology. But in this age of information, the lure of the Internet is irresistible. I include the term "mail order" in this section only because most Internet companies will allow you to send in your payments through the mail. The day of the dedicated mail order business is drawing to a close. If you really want to keep up with new materials and techniques in incense making, you need to get access to the world wide web. Most libraries offer free Internet access.

When it comes to the web, there are a wide array of businesses and groups to help you with your incense-making quest. I would recommend that you start with the list of suppliers at the end of this appendix. I have noted which of them sell the harder-to-find materials, but the web is constantly changing. Old businesses go away and many new ones arise every month. So if the list in this book doesn't provide you with the supplier you need, or if you're just curious, head to your favorite search engine. I wouldn't recommend typing in "incense" as a search word. You'll get tens of thousands of results listing the sale of poor quality dipped incense. Try "incense making," or something similar, to find general information. Be aware that many sites that list incense-making instructions have simply illegally copied information from one of the incense making books on the market. Since many of them advocate the use of saltpeter and other improper techniques, I'd take those with a huge grain of salt.

If you're looking for a specific ingredient, try typing in its name at the search engine. You can often find a company who can supply that item in just a few minutes. You might also try entering the Latin name of the ingredient in the search engine. You can often find interesting articles about ingredients by doing that. It is almost always an educational experience.

Finally, you'll also find the Internet to be a source for advice. If you are someone who enjoys chat or message groups on the web, then you'll find there are a number of them on the topics of incense and incense making. I run such a group myself and belong to many others. They are simply a font of information (although it is not always good information) but like any other chat or forum-based web activity, they are prone to disharmony. Different groups feel the need to promote agendas or dogma that they consider important. I don't think there's anything wrong with that—after all, diversity improves us all. Be aware that the answers you get to any questions posed come from a specific philosophical perspective and might not reveal all sides of the issue. Just use your own experiences and purposes to guide you. If you prefer to remain clear of entangling philosophies and politics it might be wise to merely read the messages and not add to them. Just trust yourself and the powers that guide you through life and read everything (including this book) with a critical eye.

In the United States

Abyss Distribution & Azure Green ■ 800-326-0804
P. O. Box 48 ■ Middlefield, MA 01243

Enchantments Inc. ■ 212-228-4394
341 East 9th Street ■ New York, NY 10003

FireWind Herbal Products ■ 877-950-3330
P. O. Box 5527 ■ Hopkins, MN 55343

Good Scents ■ 800-777-8027
327 Carpenters Lane ■ Cape May, NJ 08204

Grandpa's General Store ■ 608-269-0550
408 S. K Street ■ Sparta, WI 54656

Healing Waters & Sacred Spaces ■ 503-528-1430
2426 NE Broadway ■ Portland, OR 97232

The Herbal Glen ■ 918-742-6133
6508 S. Peoria Ave. ■ Tulsa, OK 74136

In Harmony Herbs & Spices ■ 800-514-3727
4808 Santa Monica Ave. ■ San Diego, CA 92107

Isis Metaphysical Books & Gifts ■ 800-808-0867
5701 E. Colfax Ave. ■ Denver, CO 80220

Magickal Enchantment Metaphysical Store ■ 877-845-9775
200 E. Dana Street, Suite #7 ■ Mountain View, CA 94041

Mother's Hearth ■ 866-835-3290
3443 E.11th Street ■ Tulsa, OK 74112-3825

Mountain Rose Herbs ■ 800-879-3337
85472 Dilley Lane ■ Eugene, OR 97405

PoTO Books & Herbs ■ 310-451-9166
1223 Wilshire Blvd. #925 ■ Santa Monica, CA 90403

Sacred Traditions ■ 425-793-8669
3510 NE 4th Street, Suite A ■ Renton, WA 98056

Scents of Earth ■ 800-323-8159
P. O. Box 859 ■ Sun City, CA 92586

Shoyeido Incense ■ 800-786-5476
1700 38th Street ■ Boulder, CO 80301

Taos Herb Company ■ 800-353-1991
P. O. Box 3232 ■ Taos, NM 87571

Two Hundred Hands ■ 866-497-4561
2808 Jefferson NE ■ Albuquerque NM 87110

In the United Kingdom

Druidskeep ■ +44 (0) 1204 304483
3 Palm Street, Astley Bridge ■ Bolton, Lancashire BL1 8PQ

Mesmerize Magickal Supplies ■ 01709 821403
26 Wellgate Rotherham ■ South Yorkshire, S60 2LR

New Moon Enterprises ■ 01235 819 744
P. O. Box 110 ■ Didcot, Oxon OX11 8YT

Appendix C:

Advanced Incense Philosophies

Once you've mastered the basics of incense making, you might want to pursue this fascinating pastime for years to come. If you do decide to become an incense maker (you never have to become a "professional" to be a skilled incense maker), then there are some ethical concerns you'll need to consider. This is especially important if you make ritual incense. If your incense-making practices don't agree with your spiritual beliefs, then the value of your incense is diminished.

Incense Making and the Environment

Incense ingredients are gifts from the Earth. Even the most common rosemary plant is a wonderful surprise and deserves proper respect. The more rare and precious the material, the more respect it deserves. That brings up the point of endangered plants and trees. Indian yellow sandalwood is endangered (although sandalwood is exported from other nations where it is rare but not necessarily endangered). It's illegal to import it into many countries. Aloeswood is also at high risk. There are plans in the works to save these species, but nothing of that nature is certain. Using these materials might hasten the demise of these rare and precious gifts.

Not all rare materials are endangered, to be sure. Some are difficult to harvest. Some plants produce only tiny quantities of the desired material, and that makes them rare and expensive (saffron is a good example). Those plants might face no threat of extinction, but merely be limited by the quantity that any one region can grow.

There is no doubt of the power held in these rare materials. It has long been understood that these precious ingredients have powers to heal and much more. They have been used in incense for thousands of years. Sadly, the love of the power in these materials may lead to their ultimate extinction. So before you decide to use one of these rare ingredients, you should consider this factor.

I'm not saying you should never use rare materials, but please consider it very carefully. Although aloeswood and others are threatened, careful management of these resources at their point of origin is the key to their survival. Support this management by only purchasing rare materials through reputable importers in your own country. If you do use rare ingredients, treat them with the greatest of respect. Don't waste one gram of this material. Once you've made incense with it, don't burn it frivolously. Save it for special occasions or rituals. You should also thank the plants that provided the rare materials. Carefully consider how your path or tradition views rare plants before using them in your incense.

"Killing" versus "Non-killing" Ingredients

Another factor that might be important in some traditions is the notion of "non-killing" ingredients. It is much like a "non-killing fast," where no food is eaten if the plant or animal that provided it had to be killed (for example, apples would be fine because the tree isn't killed, but head lettuce wouldn't be acceptable because the plant has to die). "Killing" materials are any ingredients that require the plant or tree be killed before use. Generally, woods are killing materials. Certainly, all heartwood is a killing material, but it is possible to use wood from fallen or trimmed branches that would be considered "non-killing." Although some importers do claim that their woods are non-killing, I think it's best to assume that unless you collected the wood yourself it is a killing material. Some plant materials are also of the killing variety. Most roots are killing ingredients unless very carefully collected.

On the other hand, many plants are non-killing. Plants like chamomile and lavender are harvested without any harm to the plant. Most plants whose leaves are used (like sage) are also non-killing. Resins are also non-killing materials. Frankincense, dragon's blood, and myrrh are all examples of this. The tree that provides such a valuable resin is treated with great care and respect. It can take generations for a tree to give a truly fragrant resin, so the trees are well hidden and tended with love. In fact, many groves of fragrant trees are still hidden away and the location never revealed to outsiders. The leaves and needles from trees, "runners" from larger mother plants and flowers from plants are all non-killing materials. Although this isn't a consideration for all paths or traditions, it is another important philosophy that you should consider as your incense making skills grow.

The Incense Shadow World

Sadly, there is a "shadow world" of deceit and crime that exists in the world of incense making. It ranges from time-tested methods of defrauding incense buyers with inferior products to the harvesting of animals for incense makers. It is unfortunate that these problems are significant enough to warrant discussing in this book, but everyone who uses or makes incense needs to be aware of these problems.

Fraud

For as long as there have been traders of incense, there have been those who would take advantage of their customers. This is far less of a problem with fraud on low-cost incense materials. Although there are some vendors who will mislead their customers about low-cost ingredients by "cutting" the material with cheaper ingredients, fraud is a lot of work. People don't usually want to go to all the trouble for an item that will give them three dollars' profit. Having said that, it does occasionally happen. There are some unscrupulous sellers who take any powdered wood, scent it with fragrance oils, and then sell it as aloeswood powder or sandalwood powder.

But there are some incense materials that are far more costly than gold. When it comes to this level of incense ingredient, fraud is a much larger problem. Inferior woods are sometimes soaked in oils to make them appear more valuable than they are. Sometimes a buyer who hasn't done enough research can be fooled into thinking that one kind of wood is actually another that is far more valuable. I have no doubts that the sellers who perpetrate these frauds have many more evil tricks up their sleeves.

Plunder

Even more tragic than the fraud that goes on is the plunder of the environment for profit. Although India has laws regarding the exportation and exploitation of yellow sandalwood (*Santalum album*), poaching appears to be rampant. It's impossible to say how much of the sandalwood sold in the world is actually poached Indian yellow sandalwood. All of the other protected incense materials face similar problems. Most of these materials are found in quite poor regions of the world. It is understandable why local peoples would be tempted to plunder what they see as a local resource. It is the demand by wealthy people for these materials that drive the prices so high that no poor person could resist the temptation.

As hard as it is to believe, even in the twenty-first century the exploitation of animals for their aromatic parts still continues. Although the use of animal products in incense is rare in the West, it is still an accepted practice among some in the East. Ambergris, musk oil (from numerous species), and other animal products have historically been used in incense and these practices still continue today. My biggest personal objection is that many of these animal materials are killing materials in the worst sense. Recently, I was personally shocked to see an American incense "expert" ask a group of people if they had ever experienced real musk. I certainly hope the answer for everyone was "no"! Much like the trade in ivory, the trade in animal aromatics is something we should strive to leave in the past. There are ongoing attempts in parts of the world to ranch animals and extract their musk without killing them. I really think is much like harvesting ivory from elephants and not killing them. It is a more humane method of harvesting, but it may well cause more harm than good since it will offer those who poach animals the opportunity to use the guise of "farmed animal goods" to legitimize their ill-gotten products. Please avoid the use of animal products in your incense.

Conspicuous Consumption

You might ask, and rightly so, why people are willing to pay ten times the price of gold for a small bit of wood or part of an animal. There are two different basic reasons, but they both boil down to the same thing: selfishness. The first reason is that some people who are extremely knowledgeable about incense understand how to use these substances to great effect. Absolutely wonderful incense can be produced with these materials that can offer all sorts of benefits to the user. Although I must question the karmic price that these people will have to pay for this desire to have the ultimate incense.

There is another, even sadder, reason that some people engage in the trade of these precious materials. Some people do it in order to be a part of an "elite" group. They feel the need to travel and collect as many expensive rare oils and aromatics as they can in order to impress the other members of their clique. I have met some of these people and have no doubt there are many more in nations across the world. Their drive for social acceptance (and their too-abundant cash reserves) sends them in search of these ingredients. Worst of all, they tend to collect or hoard what they do purchase, so its wonderful gift of scent is locked away from everyone and never put to any use at all. What a waste.

Both of these reasons still add up to untempered personal desire and selfishness. Whether it is a desire to collect or a desire to create the ultimate olfactory experience, it is simply self-centered. Driving prices to such outrageous levels that people will ravage their own place of birth is both irresponsible and shows disrespect to the Earth. I don't want anything you ever experience or learn from this book to lead you down this dark path. I say to these "conspicuous consumers" that the ends do not justify the means. If we one day discovered that young children had some wonderful aromatic gland in their skulls, we would still never use it for incense. There must be limits to personal desire in order to preserve the greater good.

Trust Yourself

When it comes to challenging ethical problems like these, trust yourself. Think about the situation and consider the training you've received. Then listen to what your conscience tells you. If you are unsure, ask the deities for a clearer choice. Trust yourself to know the right answer. As long as you ask yourself tough questions about what you do, you'll be true to your beliefs.

As you journey along the path of the incense maker, you might encounter people who will offer you advice that runs counter to what you believe. You might meet those who tell you that no incense materials are actually endangered. You might encounter "experts" who tell you that if you don't burn aloeswood, then you don't know what incense is actually about. You may find those who criticize your techniques of incense making or the traditions you follow. Always keep this advice in mind: remain true to your path and your beliefs but always consider what others say. Don't just close your ears and eyes—keep an open mind. Nevertheless, be true to what you know is right no matter what any "expert" might say to you.

Incense, like life, is a learning process. I tend to ignore anyone who preaches that there is only one way to understand incense (or anything else for that matter). Such dogmatic incense makers are missing much of the joy of the art through their closed-minded approach. But that doesn't mean that they don't have anything to contribute. Listen to what they have to say, extract anything useful in it and then move on.

Techniques and ingredients go beyond dogma and can be used by those of many beliefs. Incense making is an art that looks both into the past and the future. In the future, we might discover that some of the techniques in this book are inferior. That's why we work at this—to improve our abilities and our knowledge. This is accomplished by both the study of the past and research for the future. As we each learn more, we can teach one another. We have to be willing to let go of bad techniques in favor of better ones as evidence presents itself. Just because an incense maker is bogged down with dogma doesn't mean their techniques are invalid.

Just don't let any incense "experts" (or snobs or conspicuous consumers) discourage you. There is no one right way to do things and no one ingredient that makes incense perfect. Perfection, like beauty, is in the nose of the beholder. Keep an open mind, stay true to your beliefs, and you will have all the armor you need to resist any "experts" who try to tell you how wrong you are.

Incense making does require some thought to ethics. You must decide what ingredients are proper to use under your own beliefs. Don't worry about finding the rarest and most expensive incense ingredients—stick with local materials when you can. If you keep your incense natural and stay with your own ethics despite what you might see or read, you'll be rewarded with wonderful incense for the rest of your life.

Appendix D:
Suggested Ritual Uses

Before saying anything in this section, I want to offer this observation. Many spiritual traditions or paths have very specific ways of conducting rituals and using incense. The suggestions in this appendix aren't in any way intended to replace the teachings of your tradition but rather to offer ideas that could be incorporated into your normal ritual practices. If you are eclectic, as I am, then designing your own rituals (or incorporating new ideas into old rituals) is something you do regularly. In that case, using this appendix should be quite easy. In any event, these suggestions are just that—suggestions. You understand your own spiritual practices more than anyone else can. Edit or replace the words I offer, remove any parts that conflict with your normal practices or follow the rituals exactly, it is up to you. As always, trust in your inspiration.

Cleansing

This is one of the most fundamental uses for incense. Foul odors can indicate a foul presence and incense has often been used to remove both at the same time. Cleansing, or purification, is an important first step in many rituals. It is also a critical step in preparing sacred space.

Space Cleansing Ritual

I've always thought that simple rituals are the best, although the pageantry of an elaborate ritual is always a lot of fun. Use this quick ritual to clear the negative energies that often collect as a result of daily life. It's also very useful after any negative incident that might take place in your home. This quick ritual can be easily used anywhere you go.

First, select a cleansing incense. This can be anything from a simple sage to a complex cleansing recipe, but it should be a stick or cone that you've empowered for the purpose of cleansing. Grab an appropriate censer or incense burner. Begin the ritual by quieting your mind. This is most simply accomplished by slowly taking in and releasing a few deep breaths. Visualize the negative energy in the space. See the negative energy in your mind's eye. Face East and light your incense. Offer the incense to the East by holding the censer before you in both hands and lifting it above the level of your eyes. If you wish, you can add a spoken invocation as well.

"Great Spirits of Air, I ask that you cleanse this space and banish the negative energies that dwell in this place."

You can, of course, modify the invocation to fit with your own tradition or just to sound the way you wish. The important step is to visualize the negative energies flying away through the roof or out the windows. Your body might tingle a bit as the energies from your incense and energies from your person spread out, forcing the negative energies away. As you do this, also visualize the energy moving from the incense into your lungs and then moving back out again as you exhale, adding your personal energy to that of the incense.

If you are cleansing a small space, turn towards the South. If you are in a space where you can move around, walk to the Southernmost part of the room and face South. The spoken invocation might follow the form of the first one.

"Great powers of Fire, I ask that you cleanse this space and banish the negative energies that dwell in this place."

Visualize waves of heat and tiny streaks of fire streaming from the incense and eliminating any negative energies they contact.

Continue to the West and invoke the powers of Water. Visualize the negative energies being forced out by the pure energy of Water. If you are in a room with a sink, visualize the negative energies being forced out through the drain.

Finally, move to the North and invoke the powers of the Earth. Visualize the few remaining negative energies being forced out of the space through the floor or ground where you are standing. Set the censer down (in a safe location of course) and allow the incense to continue to burn until it has burned out. Once the incense has gone out, clean your censer.

Tool Cleansing

Cleansing is also a good idea whenever you acquire a new altar tool. You might find a nice chalice (cup) at an estate sale and want to cleanse it of any negative energies that might have been left by the previous owner. I even like to cleanse brand new tools. You have no way of knowing who has handled them before they arrived to you, so cleansing is a good place to start whenever you add a new tool to your altar.

123

Begin by selecting a cleansing incense. For single herb incense, I like to use rosemary for cleansing tools, but an incense blend specifically designed and empowered for cleansing is best. If you maintain a permanent altar, place your censer or incense burner on the altar. If you don't have a permanent altar, any flat workspace will do. First quiet your mind, then light the incense. Hold the tool in your hands and study it for a moment. Then see the tool in your mind's eye. Visualize it as dirty or rusty. Carefully hold the tool above the incense and slowly move it back and forth so that the smoke touches every part of the tool. As the smoke touches the tool, visualize the dirt or rust vanishing. As you turn and move the tool through the smoke, see it becoming new and shiny, even if the tool is quite old and appears battered to the naked eye.

If you want a spoken invocation, you might say:

"Cleansing incense, banish the negative energies in this [name the tool]. Make it pure and whole."

Once the tool is completely cleansed, lay it on your altar or workspace until the incense has finished burning. Once the incense has gone out, clean your censer and put your new tool away in an appropriate place.

Incense Listening Ritual

"Listening to incense" is discussed in more detail in Appendix E, but I wanted to offer this little ritual. I like to sit down and listen to a single incense ingredient from time to time. You never know what might be revealed to you. Sometimes, when I listen to a certain aromatic it tells me things that disagree with what I might have read about it. I personally sometimes use an aromatic in a different way than is generally accepted (for example, using an herb generally considered to be under the sign of Air as an Earth sign instead). Listen to what your incense says and you might be surprised.

Begin by selecting an aromatic (you can do this with bases and binders as well). You can use rolled incense, but listening is best done with just the pure aromatic so I'd use charcoal. Thank the plant that offered the aromatic and ask it to enlighten you. You might use this spoken invocation.

"Wonderful [name the herb], gift of the Earth, I ask that you open my eyes and my soul to your true spirit and tell me of your secrets."

Quiet your mind and put the aromatic on your charcoal. Close your eyes and keep your mind clear for thirty to sixty seconds. As the scent of the aromatic wafts over you, open your mind to the scent. Do any images or sensations come to your mind? How about your mind's eye?

Listening to aromatics is a skill much like listening to people. It requires practice and a sincere desire to understand. When you first begin, you might have trouble hearing what the scent is telling you. But persistence will pay off. You might want to keep a journal of your impressions of various aromatics and see how they change over time as you learn to listen more carefully.

Creating Sacred Space

Creating sacred space is a very important step for rituals and this is perhaps the area of magick where the power of incense most greatly excels. The creation of sacred space is actually preparing a welcome and pure environment into which you can invite any deities or spirits that you wish. Simply burning properly empowered incense is enough to completely change the atmosphere of a space from the mundane world to a space where magick is welcomed. Truly, no ritual is needed, but if you feel the need for one then by all means you're welcome to try this.

You can use any empowered incense for this ritual. Cleansing or altar incense would be the most appropriate, but since all empowered incense is magickal, any kind will do. You might want to use the incense you plan to use later during your ritual. Select your incense and censer. Quiet your mind. Light the incense. Begin to walk through the area you plan to use. Visualize the change in energy as you walk through the room. Everywhere you go and everything that is touched by the sacred smoke is energized and vibrant when compared to its mundane energies before the incense. If you plan to cast a magick circle in your sacred space, you should walk the perimeter (clockwise) where your circle will be cast. That way you can fully energize the air inside the circle. If you wish to have a spoken invocation, repeat these words as you walk.

"Into this space no harm shall come. From this place no harm shall go. Sacred smoke creates sacred spaces."

Continue walking through the area until you feel it is totally energized. You should be able to clearly visualize the pure energies in the space. You might see it as a bright color or dancing bolts of energy. Place your censer on your altar and allow the incense to burn out. You might use this time to lay out any altar tools you plan to use, incense for rituals, ritual clothing, etc. It is also an excellent time for a ritual bath.

Calling Quarters

If you practice rituals inside a magick circle, then you know that "calling the quarters" is an important step in establishing the circle. Rather than going into a lengthy example of calling quarters, I'll just say that incense can play a valuable part in this process. If you place a censer or burner at each of the cardinal points of your circle, you can offer a different incense to each of the quarters. You would want to empower and roll incense appropriate to the quarter being called (Water aromatics to the West, Earth aromatics to the North, etc.). If you use candles to mark your quarters, I would first light the candle and then light the incense from it.

This practice is one more good argument for making spaghetti sticks. If you use thick cylinders, sticks with rods, or even cones, having one type of incense burning at each quarter plus the incense you have on your altar, you might end up "smoking yourself out." I know that in my early studies with incense I would sometimes create such a thick pall of smoke that I couldn't see to read. By using spaghetti sticks, each stick produces a very small amount of smoke (although the scent is still quite powerful). Having four or five spaghetti sticks burning at once shouldn't create any problems.

You might also think that having so many different types of incense burning at once would create unpleasant smells. Surprisingly, the scents tend to complement each other and create a whole new scent as they meld. I call this "air mixing." It can be quite effective and fun to try. For best results, I'd use simple recipes for your quarter incense. One or two aromatics only in those blends. That way, with all four quarters burning, the scents only contain four aromatics. Many incense blends contain far more than that. The most wonderful thing about using incense at each quarter in this fashion is that as you walk around your altar inside the circle, you pass through the different "scent zones." As you walk past the Air quarter, you can "hear" the air. Also, as you walk your entire body helps to stir and mix the air inside the circle, thus blending the four scents into one.

Sanctifying Tools

Although I discussed cleansing tools earlier, this is a different ritual with a very different purpose in mind. I know that many practitioners never feel the need to take this extra step, so you might not either, but personally I enjoy it and find it most rewarding. Sanctifying serves both as a formal acknowledgment that you are adding a new magick tool to your work and also to place a personal "mark" upon the tool, claiming it as yours alone.

Begin by cleansing the tool. You could cleanse the tool days or even weeks before sanctifying it. Although not mandatory, I prefer to sanctify tools under the full moon. If you routinely cast a magick circle I would definitely suggest sanctifying tools within the circle. Select an incense. If you have a personal incense blend you like to use (it's very nice to create a scent for you and you alone—it is a way to distinguish yourself) I would use that. If not, any altar incense blend will work fine.

Begin by lighting the incense and placing it on your altar. Hold the tool in both hands and stand before your altar. Visualize the cleansed tool, shining and clean. As the smoke rises, see its energies blending with your own personal energy and flowing into the tool. As you see the energy flowing into the tool, visualize your own mark being deeply engraved into the tool. Whether that be your magickal name, your initials, your personal symbol, or any other mark you wish. If you would like to add a spoken invocation, you might say the following:

"I welcome this new tool and mark it as my own. Be it known to all powers that this tool is mine and will serve only to the good of the world and never its harm. It will serve no one but me or those I appoint."

If you are performing the ritual within a magick circle, I would then present the tool to each of the four quarters in turn before placing it back onto the altar. The tool is now yours and carries your mark. Take care who you allow to handle such altar tools after you have performed this ritual.

Special Occasions

It's always a wonderful surprise when an incense maker presents someone with a blend made just for a special occasion. Sabbats, handfastings, initiations, birthdays, or other celebrations are all excellent reasons to create a special incense blend. It will not only enhance the occasion, it will also make it extremely memorable in the minds of everyone there. Scent has a deep and lasting effect on the brain and incense can create a unique aromatic atmosphere that will leave a permanent mark. You'll find several of these recipes in chapter 7 but you should seriously consider making your own unique blend. You might want to make some extra of the blend and offer it as a gift to your host or guests. Incense can also be quite special when you make a blend for such occasions that you use strictly while alone. It is yours and yours only. That can be a special magick of its own.

Invoking Deities and Spirits

There are several ways to use incense on your altar to summon deities or spirits, but I only want to mention two of them. I call them the "one stick" and "multistick" methods. You may want to create a single type of incense for use on your altar. The scent might change each time you cast a circle or you may design a single blend that is exclusively for your altar. This is the one stick method. By that I mean that you need only burn a single incense stick on your altar.

On the other hand, if you routinely call upon multiple deities (it is quite common to call upon both a Goddess and a God in many paths, but more than two are often called) then you might want to create a special scent for each spirit or deity that you invoke. This is even more useful if you don't always call on the same spirits or deities each time. By creating a scent for each one, the presence of that incense is a special invitation for that spirit to enter your circle or aid in your magickal work. You might find that you experience the deepest connections between yourself, the spirits you invoke and the universe itself when using these spirit-specific incense blends.

127

Although the powers of the Earth and universe are always present in some form, by creating a specific blend for a specific spirit, you offer great power. Not only does it create sacred space specifically for that power, but it also creates a specific state in your own mind. The scent moves quickly to your brain and "reminds" you of the presence of that power. In the smoke of this special incense, one sometimes can see the form of the power invoked. It is a true blessing to be witness to the appearance of a God or Goddess in the smoke.

Appendix E:

"Listening to Incense" The Japanese Approach to Incense

Nowhere is the art of incense more appreciated than in Japan. Japanese incense masters are considered great artisans and are revered for their skills. Incense is deeply connected with spiritual beliefs, although there are also informal practices for the simple joy of experiencing incense. Unlike in the West, the value and wisdom of incense makers (especially those who have devoted their lives to the pursuit) is widely understood in Japan. Is it any wonder that the finest incense in the world comes from that island nation?

Listening to Incense

The Japanese masters teach that you should "listen" to incense. I find this to be a beautiful analogy that holds much truth. The word "smell" is simply inadequate to describe the sensations from experiencing incense. Before making any ritual incense, it is important to listen to your incense ingredients. By burning a single incense ingredient and listening to it carefully you can learn a great deal about it. To listen you need to quiet your own thoughts first. Then inhale the fragrant scent, hold your breath for a few seconds, and slowly exhale. The aromatic will begin speaking, or singing, to you immediately, if you are receptive to listening.

Incense as Music

I know a wise incense importer and advocate who says that incense ingredients are like individual notes in music. By learning various notes and then mastering their combination, your incense can become great music. I love this analogy as well. Much like a great musician, a great incense maker should begin learning her craft one note at a time. You might consider this book to be a primer for beginning incense "musicians." By studying your incense ingredients ("notes") one by one, you become familiar with the each of them as individuals.

Once you have learned a few notes, you can try some simple tunes. Combine two notes and then listen to the results. As you learn more and more notes, you can compose more complex tunes. The more notes you learn, the more complex your incense music can become. After seven years of incense making, I'd say that my incense sometimes whistles nice songs. There are incense masters who have listened to incense for many decades and they are able to compose magnificent symphonies. Listen to your incense and it will sing your compositions.

Makko Burning

Japanese tradition offers us an interesting alternative to burning incense on charcoal. "Makko burning" uses the same makko that is used as a binder. I should point out that makko is actually a generic term that can mean any kind of powdered incense. I don't want to devote space in this book to detailing the names of the many various Japanese incense powders, but makko is also used to describe a blend of powdered sandalwood, aloeswood, and clove. This type of makko will also work for makko burning, although it is quite fragrant on its own.

To use makko burning, you need a censer filled with ash. Traditionally, ash from rice chaff is used in Japan. You will certainly get the best results from this ash, and if you're interested in this style of burning, I'd suggest you check the list of suppliers. Many of them offer this ash and it is fairly inexpensive. It's important to note that rock or sand will not work for this method. Fill your censer 3/4 full of ash. Tamp the censer to lightly pack the ash. You then need to make an impression in the ash. Although there is a traditional U-shaped tool for this purpose, you can use a small piece of wood or the edge of a small box. You need a rectangular shape about one inch wide and three inches long. Press the wood into the ash about one inch deep. Carefully remove the wood. You can then fill the impression in the ash with makko. You then light one end of the makko. It will gradually burn from one end to the other. You can use the smoldering powder just like burning charcoal and place any aromatics you wish onto the top of the makko.

This is a novel way to burn incense and it holds it own joys, but I'm not a big supporter of this method. It has a definite place in traditional Japanese and Buddhist practices, but I don't think that the average incense user should use this method. I have no complaints about the technique itself, I just hate to see materials wasted like that. If you use makko (tabu) in your censer, then you've deprived yourself of the ability to make many cones or sticks of rolled incense. If, on the other hand, you use sandalwood, aloeswood, and clove in your censer, you've really squandered many resources. Sandalwood and aloeswood are too rare and endangered to use in place of charcoal. Save them and roll some top-quality spaghetti sticks instead. Please save your makko, whichever type you use, for incense rolling.

Bamboo Charcoal

The same tradition that offers us makko burning also offers us the ultimate alternative: bamboo charcoal. I have mentioned bamboo charcoal before because it is free of saltpeter. This charcoal is superior to any other I've ever used. Its scent is very, very subtle. It is also made of a highly renewable resource. As anyone who has ever grown bamboo will tell you, it is a hearty and plentiful plant that grows in many climates and is far from endangered. The charcoal burns well, although it is a bit slower to get started than the "self-lighting" variety. So please, leave the makko burning to incense masters and stick with bamboo charcoal as the ultimate way to burn loose or moist incense or listen to your notes. If you are interested in kodo-style burning, you will definitely need to acquire some bamboo charcoal.

The Kodo Ceremony

I want to preface this section by saying that I am not trained in kodo lore. I am presenting my own interpretation of this ancient tradition and mean no offense to those who are properly trained in this area. This is my own poor interpretation and I hope my very truncated explanation isn't too inadequate.

Kodo uses the same ash and censer that you would use for makko burning, plus you need a brick of bamboo charcoal and a mica plate. Fill your censer halfway with ash. The ash and charcoal is quite pure, so you can use the ash over and over, just sift it after each use to remove any unburned particles. Tamp the censer to lightly pack the ash. Take your charcoal brick (don't try this with "self-lighting" charcoal) and press it about halfway into the ash and carefully remove it. Then light the charcoal and allow it to burn in another censer until it is a uniform gray color. It's just like waiting for the charcoal in your grill to get to that "just right" point before you begin cooking. Put the charcoal back into the impression in the ash (using metal tongs) and add another tablespoon or two of ash. Then, carefully mound this ash around the charcoal using a butter knife, spoon, letter opener, or something similar. It's a bit like frosting a cake. The idea is to create a perfectly smooth "mountain" of ash over the top of the burning charcoal with the tip of the "mountain" in the center of the censer. Then use a large toothpick or skewer to make a hole through the tip of the "mountain" through the ash to the buried charcoal brick. A thin plate of mica tops the hole and should be pressed lightly into the ash.

Onto this highly evolved censer, a tiny bit of aloeswood is added (directly onto the mica plate). The wood is heated very gradually and the scent released without smoke. The person "listening" to the aloeswood holds the censer and partially cups his or her hand over it, places his or her face over the opening and inhales deeply through the nose. The censer is then passed from one person to the next. Different aloeswood types (truly, each individual tree smells unique) are smoldered in this way, each in its turn. This is even more evidence of the highly evolved nature of Japanese incense traditions. The incense masters understand the precious nature of aloeswood, and only the tiniest bit of wood is used each time. The masters always understand the need to hold these materials in the highest reverence.

Incense Games and Nerikoh

While kodo is a very formal ritual, the Japanese have offered a variety of secular incense practices as well. Japanese traditions have handed down a wide variety of incense games where players are allowed to listen to various woods or incense and then need to identify them later. There are many, many games in these traditions and hopefully one day we'll have a full study of them in the West. This idea is easy to apply to introducing any variety of magickal incense ingredients to the uninitiated. Simply light some charcoal, burn an aromatic, and then ask the gathered group about their impressions. Follow that with a quick explanation of the use of that aromatic. Then proceed to another aromatic. After introducing half a dozen or so aromatics, challenge them to identify the aromatics when burned a second time. You could alternatively combine two of the aromatics and challenge the group to identify which two. The idea is never to defeat the other players or for anyone to lose. The idea is for everyone to have fun and perhaps expand their minds a bit.

In the past, many of these games were played using nerikoh. I have included several nerikoh recipes in chapter 7. Some are based on traditional Japanese blends and others are new recipes with Western ingredients but made in the nerikoh form. Nerikoh is a moist form of incense that uses plum jelly or honey as a binder. It is burned on charcoal like loose incense, but it is aged to allow the scents to blend thoroughly. It's another very fun form of incense to make and I encourage you to try it.

The Japanese have given us the gift of one thousand years of research and tradition. Although ignoring much of the lore of Western incense, Japanese incense is still the most refined and developed in the world. Adapting their techniques to modern incense practices is both easy and rewarding. There are several books on the market that discuss Japanese practices and methods in far more detail. If that interests you, I'd urge you to research the topic in depth. There is also at least one formal and one informal school of Japanese incense in the United States. These groups are a font of information.

GLOSSARY

air mixing: A method of stirring the air inside a magick circle to blend various burning incense into a single scent.

altar tools: Any physical item you might use on your altar or during any magickal practices. This would definitely include cauldrons, athames, chalices, ceremonial censers, pentacles, wands, staffs, ritual bells, and candle holders.

aromatic: Any substance that produces a desirable scent when burned. Aromatics supply the majority of the aroma of any incense.

athame: A knife used in magickal practices and ritual. It is most often double-edged with a black handle. It is used to channel and focus energy and not for actual cutting.

bamboo rod: Bamboo rods or sticks are used in some incense sticks. They act to strengthen the incense and are sometimes a support for winding or rolling wet incense.

base: A base material is used in incense to improve the burning properties of the incense. Wood powder is the most common base but other materials (such as clove or evergreen needles) can be used.

binder: Binders are the "glue" that holds incense together. Many substances can be used as a binder. They are usually powdered and added to the dry mix of ingredients before adding water.

blank: An unscented stick or cone of incense. Most commercial blanks are of poor quality and aren't recommended.

boat: A type of incense burner designed to hold sticks with bamboo rods. Some are made from stone or metal and can also be used to burn spaghetti sticks.

cauldron: A round vessel with three legs. It is usually made from cast iron although pewter, brass, and stone are known to be used as well. It is often present on altars to represent the element of Water.

censer: An incense burner filled with sand, ash, or rock. It can be used to burn any form of incense. Censers are often found on altars and are an important part of some spell-work.

chalice: A cup used to hold water or ritual drinks on an altar. They range from very simple cups to elaborate drinking vessels.

cleansing: The process of removing or banishing negative energies. Cleansing is often done before using a space or a tool for magickal reasons.

coil incense: Incense coils are long spaghetti sticks that are wound around and around forming an ever-growing spiral of incense. Coils can be made to burn for many, many hours (or even days).

combination burners: An incense burner designed to hold both sticks and cones.

cone: A tapered piece of incense that is wide at the base, no thicker than an unsharpened pencil, with a flat bottom.

conspicuous consumer: A person who collects rare and expensive incense ingredients as a way to impress other people.

cultivar: A particular variety of a plant species. For example "beefsteak" and "big tom" are both tomato cultivars. Different cultivars of the same aromatic plants often have different scents.

cylinder: Round sticks of incense with no bamboo rod. Very thin cylinders are called "spaghetti sticks," but cylinders can be made as thick as an unsharpened pencil.

dipped incense: Incense made by soaking "blank" (unscented) incense in oils. The vast majority of dipped incense is made using synthetic fragrance oils. I don't recommend the use of this type of incense.

disk: An incense disk is a thin layer of incense dough cut in a circle and dried.

dough: A term for incense while it is wet. It is much like cookie dough in texture.

drying board: An unpainted, unvarnished wooden board used to hold incense as it dries. Most drying boards are flat wood, but some use channels cut into the board to keep spaghetti sticks from curling.

empowering: The transfer of energy from one item or being to another. Great magickal energies are channeled through your ritual tools (especially athames) and some of this energy can be transferred to incense when it is being made. Incense itself is empowering when burned. Empowering most commonly refers to the transfer of personal energy.

essential oil: Oil extracted from plant materials, usually through distillation. Although the oils are extracted from natural plants, the extraction process can lead to the loss of chemicals naturally found in the plant and the creation of new compounds through chemical changes. Oils should be used with care and thought in incense. You can make wonderful, natural "whole herb" incense without the use of any oils although they can certainly be included if you wish.

extruder: A tool used to force incense dough through a narrow opening in order to form solid sticks of incense.

fragrance oil: A synthetic imitation of an actual plant oil. Fragrance oils should never be used in ritual incense or incense labeled "all natural."

incense master: Someone who has dedicated her or his life to the study and perfection of incense making. Although some say that the term "master" is a masculine term, a master is someone who has mastered a skill regardless of gender. There are a significant number of women incense masters.

joss stick: This is the more traditional name for "spaghetti sticks."

killing materials: An incense making material that requires the plant providing the material to be killed in order to harvest it. Most woods are killing materials but most flowers are not.

kodo: A formal Japanese incense ceremony performed in a group.

loose incense: This term describes incense that is not "self-burning." It is called "loose" because it contains no binder to hold it together. Loose incense must be burned over a heat source, most commonly charcoal.

makko: The bark of a tree (*Machillus thunbergii*) used as a primary binder in Eastern incense. It serves as both a binder and a base material. It is also called "tabu."

makko burning: A method for burning loose incense that uses burning powder in a censer rather than using charcoal. It works fine but is not recommended because it is so wasteful of valuable natural resources.

measuring spoons: These are just like measuring spoons in the typical American kitchen. For this book you will need them in $1/8$ teaspoon, $1/4$ teaspoon, $1/2$ teaspoon, 1 teaspoon, and 1 tablespoon sizes.

mill: A grinding device used to powder incense ingredients. A mill uses a pair of flat stones to grind material to a very fine powder. Mills are how wheat is made into flour.

mind's eye: The ability to see without vision. The mind's eye is a part of imagination and allows us to "see" things even when our eyes are closed. Can you close your eyes and see your mother's face? That's seeing her in your mind's eye.

moist incense: Sometimes called "kneaded incense," it is made with honey or other unusual binders that do not dry. Moist incense is not self-burning and must have heat applied from an outside force. Some of the most ancient incense recipes are moist blends.

mortar: Usually a large and heavy bowl used for grinding. Used with a pestle.

nerikoh: An ancient Japanese form of incense. It is a "moist" form that must be aged before use.

nonkilling materials: Incense making ingredients that can be harvested without killing the plant that provided it.

pentacle: A pentagram, often raised, used on an altar as both a focal point and as a place of offering.

pestle: A tool used for grinding. The pestle is generally long and relatively thin and used in a mortar both to pound and grind incense materials.

place of power: A physical location that holds or channels magickal energy. Stonehenge is a place of power for multitudes of people. Perhaps the first place your father took you camping might be a place of power for you alone.

punk: Another term for a "blank" incense stick.

resin: The dried sap or fluid from a plant or tree. Resin is often aromatic.

ritual: I use this as a general term to refer to any magickal spell or practice—from the most elaborate spells on your altar to the simplest of magicks (such as saying "Happy birthday").

rolled incense: Incense made from herb, resin, and wood powder. The ingredients are blended and mixed with water and then rolled into sticks and cones. This is the best type of incense.

sacred space: A physical area transformed from "normal" space to a place where ritual magick can be easily performed through cleansing, energizing and the inviting of spirits and deities. The space is sacred since it is a place where Goddesses and Gods are invited.

saltpeter: Also called salt peter or saltpetre, it is a common name for potassium nitrate (or sometimes sodium nitrate). It is added to poor quality incense to try to force it to burn. It is a dangerous chemical used in making explosives and should be avoided.

self-burning incense: Incense that will burn without heat from an outside source. Cones, sticks, and coils are all examples of self-burning incense.

self-lighting charcoal: Charcoal that is made using saltpeter. It is easy to light, but it emits an unpleasant scent. This type of charcoal is not recommended.

staff: Essentially a long wand, staffs are frequently over five feet long. They are most often used in outdoor rituals.

stick incense: In this book, stick incense usually refers to incense with a bamboo rod. A different form of incense stick is called a "spaghetti stick."

spaghetti stick: A spaghetti-sized or thinner cylinder of incense without a bamboo rod. This is the ideal form for incense.

140

tree: An "incense tree" is a kind of burner designed for use with sticks with bamboo rods. Some are made from stone or metal and can also be used to burn spaghetti sticks.

visualization: The process of seeing with the mind's eye. Visualization is an important part of empowering incense and magick in general.

wand: Generally made from wood, wands are used to channel, direct, and sometimes to amplify magickal energies.

whole herb: Incense made with herbs, woods, and resins using natural binders and without added oils. This incense-making philosophy advocates using only plant materials and results in the most natural incense.

BIBLIOGRAPHY

Bedini, Silvio A. *The Trails of Time: Time measurement with incense in East Asia Shih-chien ti tsu-chi.* New York: Cambridge University Press, 1994.

Bremness, Lesley. *The Complete Book of Herbs.* New York: Penguin Studio, 1988.

Cunningham, Scott. *The Complete Book of Incense, Oils & Brews.* St. Paul, Minnesota: Llewellyn Publications, 1989.

———. *Cunningham's Encyclopedia of Magical Herbs.* St. Paul, Minnesota: Llewellyn Publications, 1985.

———. *Magical Herbalism: The Secret Craft of the Wise.* St. Paul, Minnesota: Llewellyn Publications, 1982.

Fettner, Ann Tucker. *Potpourri, Incense and Other Fragrant Concoctions.* New York: Workman Publishing Company, 1977.

Fischer-Rizzi, Susanne. *The Complete Incense Book.* New York: Sterling Publishing Co., Inc., 1998.

Junemann, Monika. *Enchanting Scents: The Secrets of Aromatherapy.* Durach-Bechen, Germany: Lotus Light Publications, 1988.

Meyer, Clarence. *Sachets, Potpourri & Incense: Recipes, etc.* Glenwood, Illinois: Meyerbooks, 1993.

Miller, Richard Alan. *The Magical and Ritual Use of Herbs*. Rochester, Vermont: Destiny Books, 1993.

Morgan, Keith. *Making Magickal Incenses & Ritual Perfumes*. London: Pentacle Enterprises, 1993.

"Occupational safety and health guideline for dipropylene glycol methyl ether" in Occupational Safety and Health Administration (OSHA) Health Guidelines database [database online]; available from http://www.osha-slc.gov/SLTC/ healthguidelines/dipropyleneglycolmethylether/recognition.html; Internet; accessed 28 June 2002.

Smith, Steven R. *Wylundt's Book of Incense*. York Beach, Maine: Samuel Wiser, Inc., 1989.

Wildwood, Chrissie. *The Bloomsbury Encyclopedia of Aromatherapy*. London: Bloomsbury Publishing Plc, 2000.

I also want to thank all the members of the Alice's Restaurant Incense List for all their articles and discussions on making incense with natural ingredients, information on Japanese incense making and burning techniques, the dangers of chemicals like DPG, saltpeter, and other chemicals commonly used in incense making. Although it is not possible to cite each one individually, their articles were important sources for this book.

INDEX

149

Spell Crafts

Creating Magical Objects

Scott Cunningham
& David Harrington

Since early times, crafts have been intimately linked with spirituality. When a woman carefully shaped a water jar from the clay she'd gathered from a river bank, she was performing a spiritual practice. When crafts were used to create objects intended for ritual or that symbolized the Divine, the connection between the craftsperson and divinity grew more intense. Today, handcrafts can still be more than a pastime—they can be rites of power and honor; a religious ritual. After all, hands were our first magical tools.

Spell Crafts is a modern guide to creating physical objects for the attainment of specific magical goals. It is far different from magic books that explain how to use purchased magical tools. You will learn how to fashion spell brooms, weave wheat, dip candles, sculpt clay, mix herbs, bead sacred symbols, and much more, for a variety of purposes. Whatever your craft, you will experience the natural process of moving energy from within yourself (or within natural objects) to create positive change.

0-87542-185-7, 224 pp., 5 ¼ x 8, illus., photos $12.95

Cunningham's Encyclopedia of Magical Herbs

Scott Cunningham

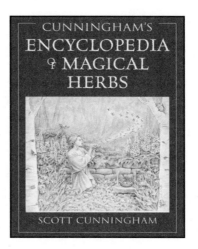

This is the most comprehensive source of herbal data for magical uses ever printed! Almost every one of the over 400 herbs are illustrated, making this a great source for herb identification. For each herb you will also find: magical properties, planetary rulerships, genders, associated deities, folk and Latin names, and much more. To make this book even easier to use, it contains a folk name cross-reference, and all of the herbs are fully indexed. There is also a large annotated bibliography, and a list of mail- order suppliers so you can find the books and herbs you need. Like all of Cunningham's books, this one does not require you to use complicated rituals or expensive magical paraphernalia. Instead, it shares with you the intrinsic powers of the herbs. Thus, you will be able to discover which herbs, by their very nature, can be used for luck, love, success, money, divination, astral projection, safety, psychic self-defense, and much more. Besides being interesting and educational it is also fun, and fully illustrated with unusual woodcuts from old herbals. This book has rapidly become the classic in its field. It enhances books such as 777 and is a must for all Wiccans.

0-87542-122-9, 336 pp., 6 x 9, illus. $14.95

The Complete Book of Incense, Oils & Brews

Scott Cunningham

For centuries the composition of incenses, the blending of oils, and the mixing of herbs have been used by people to create positive changes in their lives. With this book, the curtains of secrecy have been drawn back, providing you with practical, easy-to-understand information that will allow you to practice these methods of magical cookery.

Scott Cunningham, world-famous expert on magical herbalism, first published *The Magic of Incense, Oils and Brews* in 1986. *The Complete Book of Incense, Oils and Brews* is a revised and expanded version of that book. Scott took readers' suggestions from the first edition and added more than 100 new formulas. Every page has been clarified and rewritten, and new chapters have been added.

There is no special, costly equipment to buy, and ingredients are usually easy to find. The book includes detailed information on a wide variety of herbs, sources for purchasing ingredients, substitutions for hard-to-find herbs, a glossary, and a chapter on creating your own magical recipes.

0-87542-128-8, 288 pp., 6 x 9, illus. $14.95

Magical Aromatherapy

The Power of Scent

Scott Cunningham

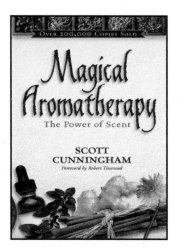

Scent magic has a rich, colorful history. Today, there is much we can learn from the simple plants that grace our planet. Most have been used for countless centuries. The energies still vibrate within their aromas.

Scott Cunningham has now combined the current knowledge of the physiological and psychological effects of natural fragrances with the ancient art of magical perfumery. In writing this book, he drew on extensive experimentation and observation, research into 4,000 years of written records, and the wisdom of respected aromatherapy practitioners. *Magical Aromatherapy* contains a wealth of practical tables of aromas of the seasons, days of the week, the planets, and zodiac; use of essential oils with crystals; synthetic and genuine oils and hazardous essential oils. It also contains a handy appendix of aromatherapy organizations and distributors of essential oils and dried plant products.

0-87542-129-6, 224 pp., illus.   **$5.99**

To order, call 1-877-NEW-WRLD
Prices subject to change without notice

Magical Needlework

35 Original Projects & Patterns

Dorothy Morrison

Creating beautiful and artistic handcrafts is in itself a magical act. Now, you can use your craft projects to further imbue your home with a magical atmosphere and evoke magical energy.

Magical Needlework explores the versatility of this magical art and offers a myriad of "hands-on" projects, ideas, and patterns submitted by a wide spectrum of people within the spiritual community. You will discover the type of magical powers contains within various symbols, numbers, shapes, textures, stitches, and weaves.

Sew a fairie dress for Midsummer Night's Eve and dancing in the moonlight . . . safeguard your home with an herbal protection charm . . . crochet a pentacle wallhanging . . . quilt an herbal soap bag and infuse it with magical success . . . knit a mediation mat for balance in your life . . . and much, much more.

1-56718-470-7, 224 pp., 8½ x 11⅞, photos, illus.   **$17.95**

Cooking by Moonlight

A Witch's Guide to Culinary Magick
Foreword by
Dana Gerhardt, Astrologer

Karri Ann Allrich

Mouthwatering temptations that feed your body and spirit

Conjure up edible pleasures for every turn of the goddess's guise—from fresh-picked herb salad and ginger-frosted pineapple cake under a sultry summer crescent, to the soul-satisfying comfort of turkey meatloaf and pumpkin soup during the cold winter moons.

Trust your body to gravitate toward the nourishment it needs most. *Cooking by Moonlight* promotes cooking with intention, in harmony with the seasons and moon phases. You'll find lunar menus, 120 recipes, tips for using herbs and spices magickally, and foods appropriate for the moon's phases.

- A cookbook of 120 delicious and nourishing recipes that flow with the seasons and the lunar year

- Beverages, appetizers, soups, breads, main dishes, side dishes and vegetables, salads, and desserts

- Each lunar month's astrological lesson is presented from an intuitive goddess viewpoint, along with a befitting menu

- Includes guidelines for stocking a moonlit pantry

- Encourages you to develop your seasonal intuition with appropriate foods, herbs, and spices for each season

1-56718-015-9, 216 pp., 7 ½ x 9 ⅛ $17.95

To order, call 1-877-NEW-WRLD
Prices subject to change without notice

Garden Witchery

Magick from the Ground Up

Ellen Dugan

How does your magickal garden grow?

Garden Witchery is more than belladonna and wolfsbane. It's about making your own enchanted backyard with the trees, flowers, and plants found growing around you. It's about creating your own flower fascinations and spells, and it's full of common-sense information about cold hardiness zones, soil requirements, and a realistic listing of accessible magickal plants.

There may be other books on magickal gardening, but none have practical gardening advice, magickal correspondences, flower folklore, moon gardening, faerie magick, advanced witchcraft, and humorous personal anecdotes all rolled into one volume.

- This master gardener and practicing Witch will inspire gardeners of all ages and experience levels

- Design, plan, and maintain many kinds of Witch's gardens, including moon, container, shade, harvest, tree and bush, groundcover, fairy gardens, and houseplant gardens

- Learn the magickal meanings of plants from the perspective of color, scent, and the language of flowers

- Includes floral and herbal spells, faerie magick, Sabbat celebrations, "Witch Crafts" (sachets, wreaths, charm bags), and a Gardening Journal

0-7387-0318-4, 272 pp., 7 ½ x 7 ½, illus. $16.95

Natural Magic

Potions & Powers
from the Magical Garden

John Michael Greer

Natural magic is the ancient and powerful art of using material substances—herbs, stones, incenses, oils, and much more—to tap into the hidden magical powers of nature, transforming your surroundings and yourself.

Not just a cookbook of spells, *Natural Magic* provides an introduction to the philosophy and ways of thought underlying the system, gives detailed information on 176 different herbs, trees, stones, metals, oils, incenses, and other magical substances, and provides dozens of different ways to put them to use in magical workings. With this book and a visit to your local herb store, rock shop, or even your backyard garden, you're ready to enter the world of natural magic!

1-56718-295-X, 312 pp., 7½ x 9⅛, illus.   **$16.95**

Practical Candleburning Rituals

Spells & Rituals for Every Purpose

Raymond Buckland

Magick is a way in which to apply the full range of your hidden psychic powers to the problems we all face in daily life. We know that normally we use only five percent of our total powers. Magick taps powers from deep inside our psyche where we are in contact with the universe's limitless resources.

Magick need not be complex—it can be as simple as using a few candles to focus your mind, a simple ritual to give direction to your desire, a few words to give expression to your wish.

This book shows you how easy it can be. Here is magick for fun; magick as a craft; magick for success, love, luck, money, marriage, and healing. Practice magick to stop slander, to learn truth, to heal an unhappy marriage, to overcome a bad habit, to break up a love affair, etc.

Magick—with nothing fancier than ordinary candles, and the twenty-eight rituals in this book (given in both Christian and Old Religion versions)—can transform your life.

0-87542-048-6, 208 pp., 5¼ x 8, illus. $7.95

To order, call 1-877-NEW-WRLD
Prices subject to change without notice